£7·50

2oolennes
not matching

HOME TRUTHS.

HOME TRUTHS.

BY THE LATE
BISHOP J. C. RYLE, D.D.

/

—

NEW EDITION.

1991

SECOND SERIES.

PUBLISHED BY
ODOM PUBLICATIONS

ROUTE 1, BOX 170
KEYSER, WEST VIRGINIA 26726

58.532

PREFACE.

The "Home Truths" of the late Bishop Ryle have already rendered excellent service in behalf of evangelical belief during the "perilous times" of the latter half of the nineteenth century. It is in the persuasion that his scriptural expositions are no less applicable to the times we live in—times that are characterised by great social unrest, repudiation of constituted authority, and indifference to the claims of Jesus Christ as ruler of the conscience—that this collection of Dr. Ryle's writings, forming the second volume of the new series, is issued.

CONTENTS.

	PAGE
THE REAL PRESENCE—WHAT IS IT?	9
ARE YOU FIGHTING?	47
JUSTIFIED,	79
RICH AND POOR,	117
THE MORNING WITHOUT CLOUDS,	149
FAITH'S CHOICE,	167
"COME OUT, AND BE YE SEPARATE,"	193
"WHAT CANST THOU KNOW?"	229

THE REAL PRESENCE:

WHAT IS IT?

THE REAL PRESENCE:
WHAT IS IT?

———•══••——

"If Thy presence go not with me, carry us not up hence."—
EXOD. xxxiii. 15.

THERE is a word in the text that heads this page which demands the attention of all English Christians in this day. That word is "presence."
There is a religious subject bound up with that word, on which it is most important to have clear, distinct, and scriptural views. That subject is the "presence of God," and specially the "presence of our Lord Jesus Christ" with Christian people. What is that presence? Where is that presence? What is the nature of that presence? To these questions I propose to supply answers.

I. I shall consider, firstly, *the general doctrine of God's presence in the world.*

II. I shall consider, secondly, *the special doctrine of Christ's real spiritual presence.*

III. I shall consider, thirdly, *the special doctrine of Christ's real bodily presence.*

The whole subject deserves serious thoughts. If we suppose that this is a mere question of controversy,

which only concerns theological partisans, we have yet
much to learn.   It is a subject which lies at the very
roots of saving religion.   It is a subject which is
inseparably tied up with one of the most precious
articles of the Christian faith.   It is a subject about
which it is most dangerous to be wrong.   An error
here may first lead a man to the Church of Rome, and
then land him finally in the gulf of infidelity.   Surely
it is worth while to examine carefully the doctrine of
the " presence " of God and of His Christ.

I. The first subject we have to consider, is *the
general doctrine of God's presence in the world.*

The teaching of the Bible on this point is clear,
plain, and unmistakable.   God is everywhere.   There
is no place in heaven or earth where He is not.
There is no place in air or land or sea, no place above
ground or under ground, no place in town or country,
no place in Europe, Asia, Africa, or America, where
God is not always present.   Enter into your closet and
lock the door : God is there.   Climb to the top of the
highest mountain, where not even an insect moves :
God is there.   Sail to the most remote island in the
Pacific Ocean, where the foot of man never trod :
God is there.   He is always near us,—seeing, hearing,
observing, knowing every action, and deed, and word,
and whisper, and look, and thought, and motive, and
secret of every one of us, and everywhere.

What saith the Scripture ?   It is written in Job,

" His eyes are upon the ways of man, and He seeth all
his goings.   There is no darkness, nor shadow of death
where the workers of iniquity may hide themselves"
(Job xxxiv. 21, 22).   It is written in Proverbs, " The
eyes of the Lord are in every place, beholding the evil
and the good" (Prov. xv. 3).   It is written in Jeremiah,
" Thine eyes are open upon all the ways of the sons of
men : to give every one according . . . to the fruit
of his doings " (Jer. xxxii. 19).   It is written in the
Psalms, " Thou knowest my downsitting and mine
uprising, Thou understandest my thought afar off.
Thou compassest my path and my lying down, and art
acquainted with all my ways.   For there is not a word
in my tongue, but, lo, O Lord, Thou knowest it
altogether. . . .   Whither shall I go from Thy
Spirit ? or whither shall I flee from Thy presence ?   If
I ascend up into heaven, Thou art there : if I make my
bed in hell, behold, Thou art there.   If I take the
wings of the morning, and dwell in the uttermost parts
of the sea ; even there shall Thy hand lead me, and
Thy right hand shall hold me.   If I say, Surely the
darkness shall cover me ; even the night shall be light
about me.   Yea, the darkness hideth not from Thee ;
but the night shineth as the day : the darkness and
the light are both alike to Thee " (Psalm cxxxix. 2-12).

Such language as this confounds and overwhelms us.
The doctrine before us is one which we cannot fully
understand.   Precisely so.   David said the same thing
about it almost three thousand years ago.   " Such
knowledge is too wonderful for me : it is high, I cannot

attain unto it" (Psalm cxxxix. 6). But it does not follow that the doctrine is not true, because we cannot understand it. It is the weakness of our poor minds and intellects that we must blame, and not the doctrine.

There are scores of things in the world around us, which few can understand or explain, yet no sensible man refuses to believe. How this earth is ever rolling round the sun with enormous swiftness, while we feel no motion,—how the moon affects the tides, and makes them rise and fall twice every twenty-four hours,—how millions of perfectly organised living creatures exist in every pint of pond-water, which our naked eye cannot see,—all these are things well known to men of science, while most of us could not explain them for our lives. And shall we, in the face of such facts, presume to doubt that God is everywhere present, for no better reason than this, that we cannot understand it ? Let us never dare to say so again.

How many things there are about God Himself which we cannot possibly understand, and yet we must believe them, unless so senseless as to be atheists! Who can explain the eternity of God, the infinite power and wisdom of God, or the works of God in creation and providence ? Who can comprehend a Being who is a Spirit, without body, parts, or passions? How can a material creature, who can only be in one place at one time, take in the idea of an immaterial Being, who existed before creation, who formed this world by His word out of nothing, and who can be everywhere and see everything at one and the same time ? Where, in a word, is there a single attribute of God that mortal man can thoroughly comprehend ? Where, then, is the common sense or wisdom of refusing to believe the doctrine of God being present everywhere, merely because our minds cannot take it in ? Well says the Book of Job, " Canst thou by searching find out God ? canst thou find out the Almighty unto perfection ? It is as high as heaven ; what canst thou do ? deeper than hell ; what canst thou know ? " (Job xi. 7, 8).

Let us have high and honourable thoughts of the God with whom we have to do while we live, and before whose bar we must stand when we die. Let us seek to have just notions of His power, His wisdom, His eternity, His holiness, His perfect knowledge, His " presence " everywhere. One half the sin committed by mankind arises from wrong views of their Maker and Judge. Men are reckless and wicked, because they do not think that God sees them. They do things they would never do if they really believed they were under the eyes of the Almighty. It is written, " Thou thoughtest that I was altogether such an one as thyself" (Psalm l. 21). It is written again, " They say, The Lord shall not see, neither shall the God of Jacob regard it. Understand, ye brutish among the people : and, ye fools, when will ye be wise ? He that planted the ear, shall He not hear ? He that formed the eye, shall He not see ? " (Psalm xciv. 7-9). No wonder that holy Job said in his best moments, " When I consider, I am afraid of Him " (Job xxiii. 15).

" What is your God like ? " said a sneering infidel one
day to a poor Christian.   " What is this God of yours
like : this God about whom you make such ado ?   Is
He great or is He small ? "   " My God," was the wise
reply, " is a great and a small God at the same time :
so great that the heaven of heavens cannot contain
Him, and yet so small that He can dwell in the heart
of a poor sinner like me."   " Where is your God, my
boy ? " said another infidel to a child whom he saw
coming out of a school where the Bible was taught.
" Where is your God about whom you have been reading ?   Show Him to me, and I will give you an
orange."   " Show me where He is not," was the
answer, and I will give you two.   My God is everywhere."   Well is it said in a certain place, " God hath
chosen the weak things of the world to confound the
things that are mighty."   " Out of the mouth of babes
and sucklings Thou hast perfected praise " (1 Cor. i. 27 ;
Matt. xxi. 16).

However hard to understand this doctrine may be, it
is one which is most useful and wholesome for our souls.
To keep continually in mind that God is always present with us, to live always as in God's sight, to act and
speak and think as under His eye,—all this is eminently
calculated to have a good effect upon our souls.   Wide,
and deep, and searching, and piercing is the influence
of that one thought, " Thou God seest me."

(a) The thought of God's presence is a loud call to
humility.   How much that is evil and defective must
the all-seeing eye see in every one of us !   How small a

part of our character is really known by man! "Man looketh on the outward appearance, but the Lord looketh on the heart" (1 Sam. xvi. 7). Man does not always see us, but the Lord is always looking at us, morning, noon, and night. Who has not need to say, "God be merciful to me a sinner?"

(b) The thought of God's presence is a crushing proof of our need of Jesus Christ. What hope of salvation could we have if there was not a Mediator between God and man? Before the eye of an ever-present God, our best righteousness is filthy rags, and and our best doings are full of imperfection. Where should we be if there was not a fountain open for all sin, even the blood of Christ? Without Christ, the prospect of death, judgment, and eternity would drive us to despair.

(c) The thought of God's presence teaches the folly of hypocrisy in religion. What can be more silly and childish than to wear a mere cloak of Christianity while we inwardly cleave to sin, when God is ever looking at us and sees us through and through? It is easy to deceive ministers and fellow-Christians, because they often see us only upon Sundays. But God sees us morning, noon, and night, and cannot be deceived. Oh, whatever we are in religion, let us be real and true!

(d) The thought of God's presence is a check and curb on the inclination to sin. The recollection that there is One always near us and observing us, who will one day have a reckoning with all mankind, may well keep us back from evil. Happy are those sons and daughters who, when they leave the family home, and launch forth into the world, carry with them the abiding remembrance of God's eye. " My father and mother do not see me, but God does." This was the feeling that preserved Joseph when tempted in a foreign land : " How can I do this great wickedness and sin against God ? " (Gen. xxxix. 9).

(e) The thought of God's presence is a spur to the pursuit of true holiness. The highest standard of sanctification is to " walk with God " as Enoch did, and to " walk before God " as Abraham did. Where is the man who would not strive to live so as to please God, if he realized that God was always standing at his right hand ? To get away from God is the secret aim of the sinner ; to get nearer to God is the longing desire of the saint. The real servants of the Lord are " a people near unto Him " (Psalm cxlviii. 14).

(f) The thought of God's presence is a comfort in time of public trouble. When war and famine and pestilence break in upon a land, when the nations are rent and torn by inward divisions, and all order seems in peril, it is cheering to reflect that God sees and knows and is close at hand,—that the King of kings is near and not asleep. He that saw the Spanish Armada sail to invade England, and scattered it with the breath of His mouth,—He that looked on when the schemers of the Gunpowder Plot were planning the destruction of Parliament,—this God is not changed.

(g) The thought of God's presence is a strong consolation in private trial. We may be driven from home

and native land, and placed at the other side of the
world; we may be bereaved of wife and children and
friends, and left alone in our family, like the last tree
in a forest : but we can never go to any place where
God is not, and under no circumstances can we be left
entirely alone.

Such thoughts as these are useful and profitable for
us all. That man must be in a poor state of soul who
does not feel them to be so. Let it be a settled principle in our religion never to forget that in every
condition and place we are under the eye of God. It
need not frighten us if we are true believers. The sins
of all believers are cast behind God's back, and even
the all-seeing God sees no spot in them. It ought to
cheer us, if our Christianity is genuine and sincere.
We can then appeal to God with confidence, like
David, and say, " Search me, O God, and know my
heart : try me, and know my thoughts : and see if there
be any wicked way in me, and lead me in the way everlasting " (Psalm cxxxix. 23, 24). Great is the mystery
of God's presence everywhere; but the true man of
God can look at it without fear.

II. The second thing which I propose to consider is
the real spiritual presence of our Lord Jesus Christ.

In considering this branch of our subject we must
carefully remember that we are speaking of One who is
God and man in one Person. We are speaking of One
who in infinite love to our souls, took man's nature, and

was born of the Virgin Mary, was crucified, dead, and buried, to be a sacrifice for sins, and yet never ceased for a moment to be very God. The peculiar " presence " of this blessed Person, our Lord Jesus Christ, with His Church, is the point which I want to unfold in this part of my paper. I want to show that He is really and truly present with His believing people, spiritually or after the manner of a spirit, and that His presence is one of the grand privileges of a true Christian. What then is the real spiritual " presence " of Christ, and wherein does it consist ?   Let us see.

(a) There is a real spiritual presence of Christ with that Church which is His mystical body,—the blessed company of all faithful people.   This is the meaning of that parting saying of our Lord to His Apostles, " I am with you alway, even unto the end of the world " (Matt. xxviii. 20).   To the visible Church of Christ that saying did not strictly belong.   Rent by divisions, defiled by heresies, disgraced by superstitions and corruptions, the visible Church has often given mournful proof that Christ does not always dwell in it. Many of its branches in the course of years, like the Churches of Asia, have decayed and passed away.   It is the Holy Catholic Church, composed of God's elect, the Church of which every member is truly sanctified, the Church of believing and penitent men and women, —this is the Church to which alone, strictly speaking, the promise belongs.   This is the Church in which there is always a real spiritual " presence " of Christ.

There is not a visible Church on earth, however

ancient and well ordered, which is secure against falling away. Scripture and history alike testify that, like the Jewish Church, it may become corrupt, and depart from the faith, and departing from the faith, may die. And why is this? Simply because Christ has never promised to any visible Church that He will be with it always, even unto the end of the world. The word that He inspired St. Paul to write to the Roman Church is the same word that He sends to every visible Church throughout the world, whether Episcopal, Presbyterian, or Congregational: "Be not high-minded, but fear: . . . continue in His (God's) goodness, otherwise thou also shalt be cut off"* (Rom. xi. 20-22).

On the other hand, the perpetual presence of Christ with that Holy Catholic Church, which is His body, is the great secret of its continuance and security. It lives on, and cannot die, because Jesus Christ is in the midst of it. It is a ship tossed with storm and tempest; but it cannot sink, because Christ is on board. Its

* "Whatsoever we read in Scripture concerning the endless love and the saving mercy which God showeth towards His Church, the only proper subject thereof is this Church which is the mystical body of Christ. Concerning this flock it is that our Lord and Saviour hath promised, 'I give unto them eternal life, and they shall never perish, neither shall any pluck them out of My hands.'"—*Hooker*, *Eccl. Polity*, *book iii.*, *ch. i. 2.*

These are wise words, and words that all Hooker's professed admirers would do well to ponder and digest. Few things are so mischievous as the common habit of applying to such mixed and corrupt bodies as visible Churches those blessed promises of perpetuity and preservation which belong to none but the company of true believers.

members may be persecuted, oppressed, imprisoned, robbed, beaten, beheaded, or burned; but His true Church is never extinguished. It lives on through fire and water. When crushed in one land, it springs up in another. The Pharaohs, the Herods, the Neros, the Julians, the bloody Marys, the Charles the Ninths, have laboured in vain to destroy this Church. They slay their thousands, and then go to their own place. The true Church outlives them all. It is a bush that is often burning, and yet is never consumed. And what is the reason of all this? It is the perpetual "presence" of Jesus Christ.

(b) There is a real spiritual "presence" of Christ in the heart of every true believer. This is what St. Paul meant when he speaks of "Christ dwelling in the heart by faith" (Ephes. iii. 17). This is what our Lord meant when He says of the man that loves Him and keeps His Word, "We will come unto him, and make Our abode with him" (John xiv. 23). In every believer, whether high or low, or rich or poor, or young or old, or feeble or strong, the Lord Jesus dwells, and keeps up His work of grace by the power of the Holy Ghost. As He dwells in the whole Church, which is His body, —keeping, guarding, preserving, and sanctifying it,—so does He continually dwell in every member of that body,—in the least as well as in the greatest. This "presence" is the secret of all that peace, and hope, and joy, and comfort, which believers feel. All spring from their having a Divine tenant within their hearts. This "presence" is the secret of their continuance in the faith, and perseverance unto the end. In themselves they are weak and unstable as water. But they have within them One who is " able to save to the uttermost," and will not allow His work to be overthrown. Not one bone of Christ's mystical body shall ever be broken. Not one Lamb of Christ's flock shall ever be plucked out of His hand. The house in which Christ is pleased to dwell, though it be but a cottage, is one which the devil shall never break into and make his own.

(c) There is a real spiritual " presence " of Christ wherever His believing people meet together in His name. This is the plain meaning of that famous saying, " Wherever two or three are gathered together in My name, there am I in the midst of them " (Matt. xviii. 20). The smallest gathering of true Christians for the purposes of prayer or praise, or holy conference, or reading God's Word, is sanctified by the best of company. The great or rich or noble may not be there, but the King of kings Himself is present, and angels look on with reverence. The grandest buildings that men have reared for religious uses are often no better than whitened sepulchres, destitute of any holy influence, because given up to superstitious ceremonies, and filled to no purpose with crowds of formal worshippers, who come unfeeling, and go unfeeling away. No worship is of any use to souls at which Christ is not present. Incense, banners, pictures, flowers, crucifixes, and long processions of richly dressed ecclesiastics are a poor substitute for the great High Priest Himself.

The meanest room where a few penitent believers assemble in the name of Jesus is a consecrated and most holy place in the sight of God. They that worship God in spirit and truth never draw near to Him in vain. Often they go home from such meetings warmed, cheered, stablished, strengthened, comforted, and refreshed. And what is the secret of their feelings? They have had with them the great Master of assemblies, even Christ Himself.

(*d*) There is a real spiritual "presence" of Christ with the hearts of all true-hearted communicants in the Lord's Supper. Rejecting as I do, with all my heart, the baseless notion of any bodily presence of Christ on the Lord's table, I can never doubt that the great ordinance appointed by Christ has a special and peculiar blessing attached to it. That blessing, I believe, consists in a special and peculiar presence of Christ, vouchsafed to the heart of every believing communicant. That truth appears to me to lie under those wonderful words of institution, "Take, eat: this is My body." "Drink ye all of this: this is My blood." Those words were never meant to teach that the bread in the Lord's Supper was literally Christ's body, or the wine literally Christ's blood. But our Lord did mean to teach that every right-hearted believer, who ate that bread and drank that wine in remembrance of Christ, would in so doing find a special presence of Christ in his heart, and a special revelation of Christ's sacrifice of His own body and blood to his soul. In a word, there is a special spiritual "presence" of Christ in the Lord's

Supper, which they only know who are faithful communicants, and which they who are not communicants miss altogether.

After all, the experience of all the best servants of Christ is the best proof that there is a special blessing attached to the Lord's Supper. You will rarely find a true believer who will not say that he reckons this ordinance one of his greatest helps and highest privileges. He will tell you that if he was deprived of it, he would find the loss of it a great drawback to his soul. He will tell you that in eating that bread, and drinking that cup, he realizes something of Christ dwelling in him; and finds his repentance deepened, his faith increased, his knowledge enlarged, his graces strengthened. Eating the bread with faith, he feels closer communion with the body of Christ. Drinking the wine with faith, he feels closer communion with the blood of Christ. He sees more clearly what Christ is to him, and what he is to Christ. He understands more thoroughly what it is to be one with Christ and Christ in him. He feels the roots of his spiritual life insensibly watered, and the work of grace within him insensibly built up and carried forward. He cannot explain or define it. It is a matter of experience, which no one knows but he who feels it. And the true explanation of the whole matter is this,—there is a special and spiritual " presence " of Christ in the ordinance of the Lord's Supper. Jesus meets those who draw near to His table with a true heart, in a special and peculiar way.

(e) Last, but not least, there is a real spiritual

C

" presence " of Christ vouchsafed to believers in special
times of trouble and difficulty. This is the presence of
which St. Paul received assurance on more than one
occasion. At Corinth, for instance, it is written, " Then
spake the Lord to Paul in the night by a vision, Be not
afraid, but speak, and hold not thy peace : for I am with
thee, and no man shall set on thee to hurt thee " (Acts
xviii. 9, 10). At Jerusalem, again, when the Apostle
was in danger of his life, it is written, " The night
following the Lord stood by him, and said, Be of good
cheer, Paul : for as thou hast testified of Me in Jerusalem,
so must thou bear witness also at Rome " (Acts xxiii. 11).
Again, in the last epistle St. Paul wrote, we find him
saying, " At my first answer no man stood with me, but
all men forsook me : I pray God that it may not be laid
to their charge. Notwithstanding the Lord stood with
me and strengthened me " (2 Tim. iv. 16, 17).

This is the account of the singular and miraculous
courage which many of God's children have occasionally
shown under circumstances of unusual trial, in every
age of the Church. When the three children were cast
into the fiery furnace, and preferred the risk of death to
idolatry, we are told that Nebuchadnezzar exclaimed,
" Lo, I see four men loose, walking in the midst of the
fire, and they have no hurt ; and the form of the fourth
is like the Son of God " (Dan. iii. 25). When Stephen
was beset by bloody-minded enemies on the very point
of stoning him, we read that he said, " Behold, I see the
heavens opened, and the Son of Man standing on the
right hand of God " (Acts vii. 56). Nor ought we to

doubt that this special presence was the secret of the fearlessness with which many early Christian martyrs met their deaths, and of the marvellous courage which the Marian martyrs, such as Bradford, Latimer, and Rogers, displayed at the stake. A peculiar sense of Christ being with them is the right explanation of all these cases. These men died as they did because Christ was with them. Nor ought any believer to fear that the same helping presence will be with him, whenever his own time of special need arrives. Many are over-careful about what they shall do in their last sickness, and on the bed of death. Many disquiet themselves with anxious thoughts as to what they would do if husband or wife died, or if they were suddenly turned out of house and home. Let us believe that when the need comes the help will come also. Let us not carry our crosses before they are laid upon us. He that said to Moses, " Certainly I will be with thee," will never fail any believer who cries to Him. When the hour of special storm comes, the Lord who walks upon the waters will come and say, " Peace : be still." There are thousands of doubting saints continually crossing the river, who go down to the water in fear and trembling, and yet are able at last to say with David, " Though I walk through the valley of the shadow of death, I will fear no evil ; for Thou art with me" (Psalm xxiii. 4).

This branch of our subject deserves to be pondered well. This spiritual presence of Christ is a real and true thing, though a thing which the children of this world neither know nor understand. It is precisely one of those matters of which St. Paul writes, "The natural man receiveth not the things of the Spirit of God, for they are foolishness unto Him" (1 Cor. ii. 14). But for all that, I repeat emphatically, the spiritual presence of Christ,—His presence after the manner of a Spirit with the spirits of His own people,—is a thing real and true. Let us not doubt it. Let us hold it fast. Let us seek to feel it more and more. The man who feels nothing whatever of it in his own heart's experience, may depend on it that he is not yet in a right state of soul.

III. The last point which I propose to consider, is the *real bodily presence of our Lord Jesus Christ.* Where is it? What ought we to think about it? What ought we to reject, and what ought we to hold fast?

This is a branch of my subject on which it is most important to have clear and well-defined views. There are rocks around it on which many are making shipwreck. No doubt there are deep things and difficulties connected with it. But this must not prevent our examining it as far as possible by the light of Scripture. Whatever the Bible teaches plainly about Christ's bodily presence, it is our duty to hold and believe. To shrink from holding it because we cannot reconcile it with some human tradition, some minister's teaching, or some early prejudice imbibed in youth, is presumption, and not humility. To the law and to the testimony! What says the Scripture about Christ's bodily presence? Let us examine the matter step by step.

(a) There was a bodily presence of our Lord Jesus Christ during the time that He was upon earth at His first advent. For thirty-three years, at least, between His birth and His ascension, He was present in a body in this world. In infinite mercy to our souls, the eternal Son of God was pleased to take our nature on Him, and to be miraculously born of a woman, with a body just like our own. He was made like unto us in all things, sin only excepted. Like us He grew from infancy to boyhood, and from boyhood to youth, and from youth to manhood. Like us He ate, and drank, and slept, and hungered, and thirsted, and wept, and felt fatigue and pain. He had a body which was subject to all the conditions of a material body. While, as God, He was in heaven and earth at the same time; as man, His body was only in one place at one time. When He was in Galilee He was not in Judæa, and when He was in Capernaum He was not in Jerusalem. In a real, true human body He lived; in a real, true human body He kept the law, and fulfilled all right-eousness; and in a real, true human body He bore our sins on the cross, and made satisfaction for us by His atoning blood. He that died for us on Calvary was perfect man, while at the same time He was perfect God. This was the first real bodily presence of Jesus Christ.

The truth before us is full of unspeakable comfort to

all who have an awakened conscience, and know the value of their souls. It is a heart-cheering thought that the "one Mediator between God and man is the man Jesus Christ;" real man, and so able to be touched with the feeling of our infirmities; Almighty God, and so able to save to the uttermost all who come to the Father by Him. The Saviour in whom the labouring and heavy-leaden are invited to trust, is One who had a real body when He was working out our redemption on earth. It was no angel, nor spirit, nor ghost, that stood in our place and became our Substitute, that finished the work of redemption, and did what Adam failed to do. No: it was one who was real man! "By man came death, by man came also the resurrection of the dead" (1 Cor. xv. 21). The battle was fought for us, and the victory was won by the eternal Word made flesh,—by the real bodily presence among us of Jesus Christ. For ever let us praise God that Christ did not remain in heaven, but came into the world and was made flesh to save sinners; that in the body, He was born for us, lived for us, died for us, and rose again. Whether men know it or not, our whole hope of eternal life hinges on the simple fact, that nineteen hundred years ago there was a real bodily presence of the Son of God for us on the earth.

(b) Let us now go a step further. There is a real bodily presence of Jesus Christ in heaven at the right hand of God. This is a deep and mysterious subject, beyond question. What God the Father is, and where

He dwells, what the nature of His dwelling-place who is a Spirit,—these are high things which we have no minds to take in. But where the Bible speaks plainly it is our duty and our wisdom to believe. When our Lord rose again from the dead, He rose with a real human body,—a body which could not be in two places at once,—a body of which the angels said, "He is not here, but is risen" (Luke xxiv. 6). In that body, having finished His redeeming work on earth, He ascended visibly into heaven. He took His body with Him, and did not leave it behind, like Elijah's mantle. It was not laid in the grave at last, and did not become dust and ashes in some Syrian village, like the bodies of saints and martyrs. The same body which walked in the streets of Capernaum, and sat in the house of Mary and Martha, and was crucified on Golgotha, and was laid in Joseph's tomb,—that same body,—after the resurrection glorified undoubtedly, but still real and material,—was taken up into heaven, and is there at this very moment. To use the inspired words of the Acts, "While they beheld, He was taken up; and a cloud received Him out of their sight" (Acts i. 9). To use the words of St. Luke's Gospel, "While He blessed them, He was parted from them, and carried up into heaven" (Luke xxiv. 51). To use the words of St. Mark, "After the Lord had spoken unto them, He was received up into heaven, and sat on the right hand of God" (Mark xvi. 19). The fourth Article of the Church of England states the whole matter fully and accurately: "Christ did truly rise again from death, and took again His body, with flesh, bones, and all things appertaining to the perfection of man's nature: wherewith He ascended into heaven, and there sitteth, until He return to judge all men at the last day." And thus, to come round to the point with which we started, there is in heaven a real bodily presence of Jesus Christ.

The doctrine before us is singularly rich in comfort and consolation to all true Christians. That Divine Saviour in heaven, on whom the Gospel tells us to cast the burden of our sinful souls, is not a Being who is Spirit only, but a Being who is man as well as God. He is One who has taken up to heaven a body like our own; and in that body sits at the right hand of God, to be our Priest and our Advocate, our Representative and our Friend. He can be touched with the feeling of our infirmities, because He has suffered Himself in the body being tempted. He knows by experience all that the body is liable to from pain, and weariness, and hunger, and thirst, and work; and has taken to heaven that very body which endured the contradiction of sinners and was nailed to the tree. Who can doubt that that body in heaven is a continual plea for believers, and renders them ever acceptable in the Father's sight? It is a perpetual remembrance of the perfect propitiation made for us upon the cross. God will not forget that our debts are paid for, so long as the body which paid for them with life-blood is in heaven before His eyes. Who can doubt that when we pour out our petitions and prayers before the throne of grace, we put them in the hand of One whose sympathy passes knowledge? None can feel for poor believers wrestling here in the body, like Him who in the body sits pleading for them in heaven. For ever let us bless God that there is a real bodily presence of Christ in heaven.

(c) Let us now go a step further. There is no real bodily presence of Christ in the sacrament of the Lord's Supper, or in the consecrated elements of bread and wine.

This is a point which it is peculiarly painful to discuss, because it has long divided Christians into two parties, and defiled a very solemn subject with sharp controversy. Nevertheless, it is one which cannot possibly be avoided in handling the question we are considering. Moreover, it is a point of vast importance, and demands very plain speaking. Those amiable and well-meaning persons who imagine that it signifies little what opinion people hold about Christ's presence in the Lord's Supper,—that it is a matter of indifference,—and that it all comes to the same thing at last, are totally and entirely mistaken. They have yet to learn that an unscriptural view of the subject may land them at length in a very dangerous heresy. Let us search and see.

My reason for saying that there is no bodily presence of Christ in the Lord's Supper or in the consecrated bread and wine, is simply this: there is no such presence taught anywhere in Holy Scripture. It is a presence that can never be honestly and fairly got out of the Bible. Let the three accounts of the institution of the Lord's Supper, in the Gospels of St. Matthew, St. Mark, and St. Luke, and the one given by St. Paul to the Corinthians, be weighed and examined impartially, and I have no doubt as to the result. They teach that the Lord Jesus, in the same night that He was betrayed, took bread, and gave it to His disciples, saying, " Take, eat : this is My body ; " and also took the cup of wine, and gave it to them, saying, " Drink ye all of this : this is My blood." But there is nothing in the simple narrative, or in the verses which follow it, which shows that the disciples thought their Master's body and blood were really *present in the bread and wine* which they received. There is not a word in the epistles to show that after our Lord's ascension into heaven the Christians believed that His body and blood were present in an ordinance celebrated on earth, or that the bread in the Lord's Supper, after consecration, was not truly and literally bread, and the wine truly and literally wine.

Some persons, I am aware, suppose that such texts as " This is My body," and " This is My blood," are proofs that Christ's body and blood, in some mysterious manner, are locally present in the bread and wine at the Lord's Supper, after their consecration. But a man must be easily satisfied if such texts content him. The quotation of a single isolated phrase is a mode of arguing which would establish Arianism or Socinianism. The context of these famous expressions shows clearly that those who heard the words used, and were accustomed to our Lord's mode of speaking, understood them to mean "This *represents* My body," and "This *represents* my blood."

The comparison of other places proves that there is nothing unfair in this interpretation. It is certain that the words "is" and "are" frequently mean represent in Scripture. The disciples, no doubt, remembered their Master saying such things as "The field *is* the world: the good seed *are* the children of the kingdom" (Matt. xiii. 38). St. Paul, in writing on the Sacrament, confirms this interpretation by expressly calling the consecrated bread, "bread," and not the body of Christ, no less than three times (1 Cor. xi. 26-28).

Some persons, again, regard the sixth chapter of St. John, where our Lord speaks of "eating His flesh and drinking His blood," as a proof that there is a literal bodily presence of Christ in the bread and wine at the Lord's Supper. But there is an utter absence of conclusive proof that this chapter refers to the Lord's Supper at all! The Lord's Supper had not been instituted, and did not exist, till at least a year after these words were spoken. Enough to say that the great majority of Protestant commentators altogether deny that the chapter refers to the Lord's Supper, and that even some Romish commentators on this point agree with them. The eating and drinking here spoken of are the eating and drinking of faith, and not a bodily action.

Some people fancy that St. Paul's words to the Corinthians, "The bread which we break, is it not the communion of the body of Christ?" (1 Cor. x. 16), are enough to prove a bodily presence of Christ in the Lord's Supper. But unfortunately for their argument, St. Paul does not say, "The bread is the body," but the "communion of the body." And the obvious sense of the words is this: "The bread that a worthy communicant eats in the Lord's Supper is a means whereby his soul holds communion with the body of Christ." Nor do I believe that more than this can be got out of the words.

Above all, there remains the unanswerable argument that if our Lord was actually holding His own body in His hands, when He said of the bread, "This is My body," His body must have been a different body to that of ordinary men. Of course if His body was not a body like ours, His real and proper "humanity" is at an end. At this rate the blessed and comfortable doctrine of Christ's entire sympathy with His people, arising from the fact that He is really and truly man, would be completely overthrown and fall to the ground.

Finally, if the body with which our blessed Lord ascended up into heaven can be in heaven, and on earth, and on ten thousand communion-tables at one and the same time, it cannot be a real human body at all. Yet that He did ascend with a real human body, although a glorified body, is one of the prime articles of the Christian faith, and one that we ought never to let go! Once admit that a body can be present in two places at once, and you cannot prove that it is a body at all. Once admit that Christ's body can be present at God's right hand and on the communion-table at the same moment, and it cannot be the body which was born of the Virgin Mary and crucified upon the cross. From such a conclusion we may well draw back with horror and dismay. Well says the Prayer-book of the Church of England: "The sacramental bread and wine remain still in their very natural substances, and therefore may not be adored (for that were idolatry, to be abhorred of all faithful Christians); and the natural body and blood of our Saviour Christ are in heaven, and *not here;* it being against the truth of Christ's natural body to be at one time in more places than one." This is sound speech that cannot be condemned. Well would it be for the Church of England if all Churchmen would read, mark, learn, and inwardly digest what the Prayer-book teaches about Christ's presence in the Lord's Supper.

If we love our souls and desire their prosperity, let us be very jealous over our doctrine about the Lord's Supper. Let us stand fast on the simple teaching of Scripture, and let no one drive us from it under the pretence of increased reverence for the ordinance of Christ. Let us take heed, lest under confused and mystical notions of some inexplicable presence of Christ's body and blood under the form of bread and wine, we find ourselves unawares heretics about Christ's human nature. Next to the doctrine that Christ is not God, but only man, there is nothing more dangerous than the doctrine that Christ is not man, but only God. If we would not fall into that pit, we must hold firmly that there can be no literal presence of Christ's body in the Lord's Supper; because His body is in heaven, and not on earth, though as God He is everywhere.[*]

(d) Let us now go one step further, and bring our whole subject to a conclusion. There will be a real bodily presence of Christ when He comes again the second time to judge the world. This is a point about which the Bible speaks so plainly that there is no room left for dispute or doubt. When our Lord had ascended up before the eyes of His disciples, the angels said to them, "This same Jesus, which is taken up from you into heaven, shall so come in like manner as ye have seen Him go into heaven" (Acts i. 11). There can be no mistake about the meaning of these words. Visibly and bodily our Lord left the world, and visibly and bodily He will return in the day which is emphatically called the day of "His appearing" (1 Peter i. 7).

The world has not yet done with Christ. Myriads talk and think of Him as of One who did His work in the world and passed on to His own place, like some

---

[*] The following sentence from Hooker, on the subject of Christ's body, deserves special attention :

"It behoveth us to take great heed, lest while we go about to maintain the glorious deity of Him which is man, we leave Him not the true bodily substance of a man. According to Augustine's opinion, that majestical body which we make to be everywhere present, doth thereby cease to have the substance of a true body."—*Hooker, Eccles. Polity, book v., ch. 55.*

statesman or philosopher, leaving nothing but His memory behind Him. The world will be fearfully undeceived one day. That same Jesus who came nineteen centuries ago in lowliness and poverty, to be despised and crucified, shall come again one day in power and glory, to raise the dead and change the living, and to reward every man according to his works. The wicked shall see that Saviour whom they despised, but too late, and shall call on the rocks to fall on them and hide them from the face of the Lamb. Those solemn words which Jesus addressed to the High Priest the night before His crucifixion shall at length be fulfilled: " Ye shall see the Son of Man sitting on the right hand of power, and coming in the clouds of heaven" (Matt. xxvi. 64). The godly shall see the Saviour whom they have read of, heard of, and believed, and find, like the Queen of Sheba, that the half of His goodness had not been known. They shall find that sight is far better than faith, and that in Christ's actual presence is fulness of joy.

This is the real bodily presence of Christ, for which every true-hearted Christian ought daily to long and pray. Happy are those who make it an article of their faith, and live in the constant expectation of a second personal advent of Christ. Then, and then only, will the devil be bound, the curse be taken off the earth, the world be restored to its original purity, sickness and death be taken away, tears be wiped from all eyes, and the redemption of the saint, in body as well as soul, be completed. " It doth not yet appear what we

shall be; but we know that, when He shall appear,
we shall be like Him; for we shall see Him as He is"
(1 John iii. 2). The highest style of Christian is the
man who desires the real presence of his Master, and
" loves His appearing" (2 Tim. iv. 8).

I have now unfolded, as far as I can in a short paper,
the truth about the presence of God and His Christ.
I have shown (1) the general doctrine of God's presence
everywhere; (2) the Scriptural doctrine of Christ's real,
spiritual presence; (3) the Scriptural doctrine of
Christ's real, bodily presence. I now leave the whole
subject with a parting word of application, and commend it to serious attention. In an age of hurry and
bustle about secular things, in an age of wretched strife
and controversy about religion, I entreat men not to
neglect the great truths which these pages contain.

(1) What do we know of Christ ourselves? We
have heard of Him thousands of times. We call ourselves Christians. But what do we know of Christ
experimentally, as our own personal Saviour, our own
Priest, our own Friend, the Healer of our conscience,
the comfort of our heart, the Pardoner of our sins, the
Foundation of our hope, the confidence of our souls?
How is it?

(2) Let us not rest till we feel Christ "present" in
our own hearts, and know what it is to be one with
Christ and Christ in us. This is real religion. To live
in the habit of looking backward to Christ on the cross,
upward to Christ at God's right hand, and forward to
Christ coming again,—this is the only Christianity

which gives comfort in life and good hope in death. Let us remember this.

(3) Let us beware of holding erroneous views about the Lord's Supper, and especially about the real nature of Christ's "presence" in it. Let us not so mistake that blessed ordinance, which was meant to be our soul's meat, as to turn it into our soul's poison. There is no sacrifice in the Lord's Supper, no sacrificing priest, no altar, no bodily "presence" of Christ in the bread and wine. These things are not in the Bible, and are dangerous inventions of man, leading on to superstition. Let us take care.

(4) Let us keep continually before our minds the second advent of Christ, and that real "presence" which is yet to come. Let our loins be girded, and our lamps burning, and ourselves like men daily waiting for their Master's return. Then, and then only, shall we have all the desires of our souls satisfied. Till then the less we expect from this world the better. Let our daily cry be, "Come, Lord Jesus."

NOTE.

Controversy about the Lord's Supper and the real presence of Christ, we all know, is at this moment one of the chief causes of division and disturbance in the Church of England. At such a crisis, it may not be uninteresting to some readers to hear the opinions of some of our well-known English divines about the points in dispute, in addition to those which I have already given at the end of the paper on the " Lord's Supper."

I will give four quotations from four men of no mean authority, and ask the reader to consider them.

(1) Waterland says:—

" The words of the Church Catechism, *verily and indeed taken and received by the faithful,* are rightly interpreted of a real participation of the benefits purchased by Christ's death.   The body and blood of Christ are taken and received by the faithful, not corporally, not internally, but verily and indeed, that is, *effectually.* The sacred symbols are no bare signs, no untrue figures of a thing absent; but the force, the grace, the virtue, and benefit of Christ's body broken and blood shed, that is of His passion, are really and effectually present with all them that receive worthily.   This is *all the real presence* that our Church teaches."— *Waterland's Works.*   Oxford: 1843.   Vol. vi., p. 42.

(2) Dean Aldrich, of Christ Church, says:—

" The Church of England has wisely forborne to use the term of of ' Real Presence ' in all the books that are set forth by her authority.   We neither find it recommended in the Liturgy, nor the Articles, nor the Homilies, nor the Church's Catechism, nor Nowell's. For although it be seen in the Liturgy, and once more in the Articles of 1552, it is mentioned in both places as a phrase of the Papists, and rejected for the abuse of it. So that *if any Church of England man use it, he does more than the Church directs him. If any reject it, he has the Church's example to warrant him; and it would very much contribute to the peace of Christendom if all men would write after so excellent a copy,"*—Dean Aldrich's *" Reply to Two Discourses."* Oxford: 1682. 4to., pp. 13-18.

(3) Henry Philpotts, Bishop of Exeter, in his letter to Charles Butler, says :—

" The Church of Rome holds that the body and blood of Christ are present under the accidents of bread and wine; the Church of England holds that their real presence is in the *soul of the communicant* at the Sacrament of the Lord's Supper.

" She holds, that after the consecration of the bread and wine they are changed not in their nature but in their *use*; that instead of nourishing our bodies only, they now are instruments by which, when worthily received, God gives to our souls the body and blood of Christ to nourish and sustain them: that this is not a fictitious, or imaginary exhibition of our crucified Redeemer to us, but a real though spiritual one, more real, indeed, because more effectual, than the carnal exhibition and manducation of Him could be (for the flesh profiteth nothing).

" In the same manner, then, as our Lord Himself said, ' I am the *true* bread that came down from heaven ' (not meaning thereby that He was a lump of baked dough or manna, but the true means of sustaining the true life of man, which is spiritual, not corporeal), so in the Sacrament, to the worthy receiver of the consecrated elements, though in their nature mere bread and wine, are yet, given truly, really, and effectively, the crucified body and blood of Christ; that body and blood which were the instruments of man's redemption, and upon which our spiritual life and strength solely depend. It is in this sense that the crucified Jesus is present in the Sacrament of His Supper, not in, nor with, the bread and wine, nor under their accidents, but in the souls of communicants; not carnally, but effectually and faithfully, and therefore most really."—*Philpott's Letter to Butler.* 8vo. Edition. 1825. pp. 235, 236.

(4). Archbishop Longley says, in his last Charge, printed and published after his death in 1868 :—

"The doctrine of the Real Presence is, *in one sense*, the doctrine of the Church of England. She asserts that the body and blood of Christ are 'verily and indeed taken and received by the faithful in the Lord's Supper.' And she asserts equally that *such presence is not material or corporal*, but that Christ's body 'is given, taken, and eaten in the Supper, only after a heavenly and spiritual manner' (Article xxviii.). Christ's presence is effectual for all those intents and purposes for which His body was broken and His blood shed. *As to a presence elsewhere than in the heart of a believer, the Church of England is silent*, and the words of Hooker therefore represent her views, 'The real presence of Christ's most blessed body and blood is not to be sought in the Sacrament, but in the worthy receiver of the Sacrament.'"

I will now conclude the whole subject with the following remarkable quotation, which I commend to the special attention of all my readers. It is taken from the recent elaborate judgment delivered by the Judicial Committee of the Privy Council, the highest court of the realm, in the famous case of Sheppard *v.* Bennett :—

"Any presence of Christ in the Holy Communion, which is not a *presence* to the soul of the faithful receiver, the Church of England does not by her Articles and Formularies affirm, or require her ministers to accept. This cannot be stated too plainly."

ARE YOU FIGHTING?

ARE YOU FIGHTING?

"Fight the good fight of faith" (1 Timothy vi. 12).

IT is a curious fact that there is no subject about which most people feel such deep interest as "fighting." Young men and maidens, old men and little children, high and low, rich and poor, learned and unlearned, all feel a deep interest in wars, battles, and fighting.

This is a simple fact, whatever way we may try to explain it. We should call that Englishman a dull fellow who cared nothing about the story of Waterloo, or Inkermann, or Balaclava, or Lucknow. We should think that heart cold and stupid which was not moved and thrilled by the events at Sedan, and Strasburg, and Metz, and Paris.

But, reader, there is another warfare of far greater importance than any war that was ever waged by man. It is a warfare which concerns not two or three nations only, but every Christian man and woman born into the world. The warfare I speak of is the spiritual warfare. It is the fight which every one who would be saved must fight about his soul.

This warfare, I am aware, is a thing of which many know nothing. Talk to them about it, and they are ready to set you down as a madman, an enthusiast, or a fool. And yet it is as real and true as any war the world has ever seen. It has its hand-to-hand conflicts and its wounds. It has its watchings and fatigues. It has its sieges and assaults. It has its victories and its defeats. Above all, it has *consequences* which are awful, tremendous, and most peculiar. In earthly warfare the consequences to nations are often temporary and remediable. In the spiritual warfare it is very different. Of that warfare, the consequences, when the fight is over, are unchangeable and eternal.

Reader, it is of this warfare that St. Paul spake to Timothy, when he wrote those burning words: "Fight the good fight of faith; lay hold on eternal life." It is of this warfare that I want to speak to you to-day. We meet each other at a critical period of the world's history. Men's minds are full of "wars and rumours of wars." Men's hearts are full of fear while they look at the things which seem coming on the earth. On every side the horizon looks black and gloomy. Who can tell when the storm will burst? Give me your attention for a few moments, while I try to impress on you the solemn words which the Holy Ghost taught St. Paul to write down: "Fight the good fight of faith."

1. The first thing I have to say is this: *True Christianity is a fight.*

True Christianity! Mind that word "true." Let

there be no mistake about my meaning. There is a vast quantity of religion current in the world which is not true, genuine Christianity. It passes muster; it satisfies sleepy consciences; but it is not good money. It is not the real thing which was called Christianity eighteen hundred years ago. There are thousands of men and women who go to churches and chapels every Sunday, and call themselves Christians. Their names are in the baptismal register. They are reckoned Christians while they live. They are married with a Christian marriage-service. They are buried as Christians when they die. But you never see any "fight" about their religion! Of spiritual strife, and exertion, and conflict, and self-denial, and watching, and warring they know literally nothing at all. Such Christianity may satisfy man, and those who say anything against it may be thought very hard and uncharitable; but it certainly is not the Christianity of the Bible. It is not the religion which the Lord Jesus founded, and His Apostles preached. True Christianity is "a fight."

The true Christian is called to be a soldier, and must behave as such from the day of his conversion to the day of his death. He is not meant to live a life of religious ease, indolence, and security. He must never imagine for a moment that he can sleep and dose along the way to heaven, like one travelling in an easy carriage. If he takes his standard of Christianity from the children of this world he may be content with such notions; but he will find no coun-

tenance for them in the Word of God. If the Bible
is the rule of his faith and practice, he will find his
lines laid down very plainly in this matter. He must
"fight."

With whom is the Christian soldier meant to fight?
Not with other Christians. Wretched indeed is that
man's idea of religion who fancies that it consists in
perpetual controversy. He who is never satisfied
unless he is engaged in some strife between church
and church, chapel and chapel, sect and sect, party
and party, knows nothing yet as he ought to know.
Never is the cause of sin so helped as when Christians
waste their strength in quarrelling with one another,
and spend their time in petty squabbles.

No, indeed! The principal fight of the Christian
is with the world, the flesh, and the devil. These are
his never-dying foes. These are the three chief
enemies against whom he must wage war. Unless
he gets the victory over these three, all other victories
are useless and vain. If he had a nature like an
angel, and were not a fallen creature, the warfare
would not be so essential. But with a corrupt heart,
a busy devil, and an ensnaring world, he must either
"fight" or be lost.

He must fight *the flesh*. Even after conversion he
carries within him a nature prone to evil, and a heart
weak and unstable as water. To keep that heart
from going astray, there is need of a daily struggle
and a daily wrestling in prayer. "I keep under my
body," cries St. Paul, "and bring it into subjection."

"I see a law in my members warring against the law of my mind, and bringing me into captivity." "O wretched man that I am, who shall deliver me from the body of this death?" "They that are Christ's have crucified the flesh with the affections and lusts." "Mortify your members which are upon the earth" (1 Cor. ix. 27 ; Rom. vii. 23, 24; Gal. v. 24 ; Coloss. iii. 5).

He must fight *the world*. The subtle influence of that mighty enemy must be daily resisted, and without a daily battle can never be overcome. The love of the world's good things, the fear of the world's laughter or blame, the secret desire to keep in with the world, the secret wish to do as others in the world do, and not to run into extremes—all these are spiritual foes which beset the Christian continually on his way to heaven, and must be conquered. "The friendship of the world is enmity with God: whosoever therefore will be a friend of the world, is the enemy of God." "If any man love the world, the love of the Father is not in him." "The world is crucified unto Me, and I unto the world." "Whatsoever is born of God overcometh the world." "Be not conformed to this world" (James iv. 4 ; 1 John ii. 15 ; Gal. vi. 14 ; 1 John v. 4 ; Rom. xii. 2).

He must fight *the devil*. That old enemy of mankind is not dead. Ever since the fall of Adam and Eve he has been going to and fro in the earth, and walking up and down in it, and striving to compass one great end—the ruin of man's soul. Never slumbering and never sleeping, he is always going about as a lion seeking whom he may devour. An unseen enemy, he is always near us, about our path and about our bed, and spying out all our ways. A murderer and a liar from the beginning, he labours night and day to cast us down to hell. Sometimes by leading into superstition, sometimes by suggesting infidelity, sometimes by one kind of tactics and sometimes by another, he is always carrying on a campaign against our souls. "Satan hath desired to have you, that he may sift you as wheat." This mighty adversaiy must be daily resisted if we wish to be saved. But "this kind goeth not out" but by watching and praying, and putting on the whole armour of God. The strong man armed will never be kept out of our hearts without a daily battle. (Job i. 7; 1 Peter v. 8; John viii. 44; Luke xxii. 31; Ephes. vi. 11).

Reader, perhaps you think these statements too strong. You fancy that I am going too far, and laying on the colours too thickly. You are secretly saying to yourself, that men and women in England may surely get to heaven without all this trouble and warfare and fighting. Listen to me for a few minutes, and I will show you that I have something to say on God's behalf. Remember the maxim of the wisest general that ever lived in England: "In time of war it is the worst mistake to underrate your enemy, and try to make a little war." This Christian warfare is no light matter. Give me your attention and consider what I say.

What saith the Scripture? "Fight the good fight of faith, lay hold on eternal life." "Endure hardness, as a good soldier of Jesus Christ." "Put on the whole armour of God, that ye may be able to stand against the wiles of the devil. For we wrestle not against flesh and blood, but against principalities, against powers, against the rulers of the darkness of this world, against spiritual wickedness in high places. Wherefore take unto you the whole armour of God, that you may be able to withstand in the evil day, and having done all, to stand." "Strive to enter in at the strait gate." "Labour for the meat that endureth unto everlasting life." "Think not that I am come to send peace on the earth: I came not to send peace, but a sword." "He that hath no sword, let him sell his garment, and buy one." "Watch ye, stand fast in the faith, quit you like men, be strong." "War a good warfare; holding faith, and a good conscience" (1 Tim. vi. 12; 2 Tim. ii. 3; Ephes. vi. 11-13; Luke xiii. 24; John vi. 27; Matt. x. 34; Luke xxii. 36; 1 Cor. xvi. 13; 1 Tim. i. 18, 19). Words such as these appear to me clear, plain and unmistakable. They all teach one and the same great lesson, if we are willing to receive it. That lesson is, that true Christianity is a struggle, a fight, and a warfare.

What says the Baptismal Service of the Church of England? No doubt that service is uninspired, and like every uninspired composition, it has its defects, but to the millions of people all over the globe, who

profess and call themselves English Churchmen, its
voice ought to speak with some weight. And what
does it say ?   It tells us that over every new member
who is admitted into the Church of England the
following words are used: "I baptize thee in the
name of the Father, the Son, and the Holy Ghost."
"I sign this child with the sign of the cross, in token
that hereafter he shall not be ashamed to confess the
faith of Christ crucified, and manfully to fight under
His banner against sin, the world, and the devil, and
to continue Christ's faithful soldier and servant unto
his life's end."   Of course we all know that in myriads
of cases baptism is a mere form, and that parents
bring their children to the font without faith or
prayer or thought, and receive no blessing.   The man
who supposes that baptism in such cases acts mechani-
cally, like a medicine, and that godly and ungodly,
praying and prayerless parents all alike get the same
benefit for their children, must be in a strange state of
mind.   But one thing at any rate is very certain.
Every baptized Churchman is by his profession a
"soldier of Jesus Christ," and is pledged "to fight
under His banner against sin, the world, and the
devil."   He that doubts it had better take up his
Prayer-book, and read, and mark, and learn its con-
tents.   The worst thing about many very zealous
Churchmen is their total ignorance of what their own
Prayer-book contains.

Reader, whether you are a Churchman or not, one
thing is very certain, this Christian warfare is a sub-

ject of vast importance. It is not a matter like Church government and ceremonial, about which men may differ, and yet reach heaven at last. Necessity is laid upon us. There are no promises in the Lord Jesus Christ's Epistles to the Seven Churches, except to those who "overcome."

It is a fight of *absolute necessity*. Think not that in this war you can remain neutral and sit still. Such a line of action may be possible in the strife of nations, but it is utterly impossible in that conflict which concerns the soul. The boasted policy of non-interference, the "masterly inactivity" which pleases so many statesmen, the plan of keeping quiet and letting things alone—all this will never do in the Christian warfare. Here at any rate no one can escape under the plea that he is "a man of peace." To be at peace with the world, the flesh, and the devil, is to be at enmity with God, and in the broad way that leadeth to destruction. We have no choice or option. We must either fight or be lost.

It is a fight of *universal necessity*. No rank, or class, or age, can plead exemption, or escape the battle. Ministers and people, preachers and hearers, old and young, high and low, rich and poor, gentle and simple, kings and subjects, landlords and tenants, learned and unlearned, all alike must carry arms and go to war. All have by nature a *heart* full of pride. unbelief, sloth, worldliness, and sin. All are living in a *world* beset with snares, traps, and pitfalls for the soul. All have near them a busy, restless, malicious

E

devil. All, from the king in his palace down to the pauper in the workhouse, all must fight if they would be saved.

It is a fight of *perpetual necessity.* It admits of no breathing time, no armistice, no truce. On weekdays as well as on Sundays, in private as well as in public, at home by the family fireside as well as abroad, in little things like the management of tongue and temper, as well as in great ones like the government of kingdoms—the Christian's warfare must unceasingly go on. The foe we have to do with keeps no holidays, never slumbers, and never sleeps. So long as we have breath in our bodies we must keep on our armour, and remember we are on the enemy's ground. "Even on the brink of Jordan," said a dying saint, "I find Satan nibbling at my heels." We must fight till we die.

Reader, consider well what I have been saying. Take care that your own personal religion is real, genuine, and true. The saddest symptom about many so-called Christians, is the utter absence of anything like conflict and fight in their Christianity. They eat, they drink, they dress, they work, they amuse themselves, they get money, they spend money, they go through a scanty round of formal religious services once every week. But of the great spiritual warfare —its watchings and strugglings, its agonies and anxieties, its battles and contests—of all this they appear to know nothing at all. Take care that this case is not your own. The worst state of soul is when the "strong man armed keepeth his palace, and his goods are at peace," when he leads men and women "captive at his will," and they make no resistance. The worst chains are those which are neither felt nor seen by the prisoner. (Luke xi. 21; 2 Tim. ii. 26).

Reader, take comfort about your soul, if you know anything of an inward fight and conflict. It is not everything, I am well aware, but it is something. Do you find in your heart of hearts a spiritual struggle? Do you feel anything of the flesh lusting against the spirit and the spirit against the flesh, so that you cannot do the things you would? (Gal. v. 17). Are you conscious of two principles within you, contending for the mastery? Do you see anything of war in your inward man? Well, thank God for it! It is a good sign. It is evidence not to be despised. Anything is better than apathy, stagnation, deadness, and indifference. You are in a better state than many. The most part of so-called Christians have no feeling at all. You are evidently no friend of Satan. Like the kings of this world, he wars not against his own subjects. The very fact that he assaults you, should fill your mind with hope. Reader, I say again, take comfort. The child of God has two great marks about him, and of these two you have one. HE MAY BE KNOWN BY HIS INWARD WARFARE, AS WELL AS BY HIS INWARD PEACE.

II. I pass on to the second thing which I have to say, in handling my subject: *True Christianity is the fight of faith.*

In this respect the Christian warfare is utterly unlike the conflicts of this world. It does not depend on the strong arm, the quick eye, or the swift foot. It is not waged with carnal weapons, but with spiritual. Faith is the hinge on which victory turns. Success depends entirely on believing.

A general faith in the truth of God's written Word is the primary foundation of the Christian soldier's character. He is what he is, does what he does, thinks as he thinks, acts as he acts, hopes as he hopes, behaves as he behaves, for one simple reason—he believes certain propositions revealed and laid down in Holy Scripture. "He that cometh to God must believe that He is, and that He is a rewarder of them that diligently seek Him" (Heb. xi. 6).

A religion without doctrine or dogma, is a thing which many are fond of talking of in the present day. It sounds very fine at first. It looks very pretty at a distance. But the moment you sit down to examine and consider it, you will find it a simple impossibility. You might as well talk of a body without bones and sinews. No man will ever be anything or do anything in religion, unless he believes something. Even those who profess to hold the miserable and uncomfortable views of the Deists are obliged to confess that they believe something. With all their bitter sneers against dogmatic theology and Christian credulity, as they call it, they themselves have a kind of faith.

As for true Christians, faith is the very backbone of their spiritual existence. No one ever fights earnestly against the world, the flesh, and the devil, unless he has engraven on his heart certain great principles which he believes. What they are he may hardly know, and certainly not be able to define or write down. But there they are, and consciously or unconsciously they form the roots of his religion. Wherever you see a man, whether rich or poor, learned or unlearned, wrestling manfully with sin, and trying to overcome it, you may depend there are certain great principles which this man believes. The poet who wrote the famous lines:

> "For modes of faith let graceless zealots fight,
>   He can't be wrong whose life is in the right,"

was a clever man, but a poor divine. There is no such thing as right living without faith and believing.

A special faith in our Lord Jesus Christ's person, work, and office, is the life, heart, and mainspring of the Christian soldier's character.

He sees by faith an unseen Saviour, who loved him, gave Himself for him, paid his debts for him, bore his sins, carried his transgressions, rose again for him, and appears in heaven for him as his Advocate at the right hand of God. Seeing this Saviour and trusting in Him, he feels peace and hope, and willingly does battle against the foes of his soul.

He sees his own many sins—his weak heart, a tempting world, a busy devil, and if he looked only at them he might well despair. But he sees also a mighty Saviour, an interceding Saviour, a sympathizing Saviour—His blood, His righteousness, His everlasting priesthood—and he believes that all this is his own. Believing this, he cheerfully fights on, with a full confidence that he will prove "more than conqueror through Him that loved him."

Habitual lively faith in Christ's presence and readiness to help is the secret of the Christian soldier fighting successfully.

It must never be forgotten that faith admits of degrees. All men do not believe alike, and even the same person has his ebbs and flows of faith, and believes more heartily at one time than another. According to the degree of his faith the Christian fights well or ill, wins victories, or suffers occasional repulses, comes off triumphant, or loses a battle. He that has most faith will always be the happiest and most comfortable soldier. Nothing makes the anxieties of warfare sit so lightly on a man as the assurance of Christ's love and God's protection. Nothing enables him to bear the fatigue of watching, struggling, and wrestling against sin, like the indwelling confidence that God is on his side and success is sure. It is the "shield of faith" which quenches all the fiery darts of the wicked one. It is the man who can say: "I know whom I have believed," who can say in time of suffering: "I am not ashamed."

He who wrote those glowing words: "We faint not," "Our light affliction, which is but for a moment, worketh for us a far more exceeding and eternal weight of glory," was the man who wrote with the same pen, "We look not at the things which are seen, but at the things which are not seen; for the things which are seen are temporal, but the things which are not seen are eternal" (Ephes. vi. 16 ; 2 Tim. i. 12; 2 Cor. iv. 17, 18). The more faith the more victory! The more faith the more inward peace!

Reader, I think it impossible to overrate the value and importance of faith. Well may the Apostle Peter call it "precious" (2 Peter i. 1). Time would fail me if I tried to recount a hundredth part of the victories which by faith Christian soldiers have obtained.

Take down your Bible and read with attention the eleventh chapter of the Epistle to the Hebrews. Mark the long list of worthies whose names are thus recorded, from Abel down to Moses. Note well what battles they won against the world, the flesh, and the devil. And then remember that *believing* did it all. "By it (faith) the elders obtained a good report" (Heb. xi. 2).

Turn to the pages of early Church history. See how the primitive Christians held fast their religion even unto death, and were not shaken by the fiercest persecutions of heathen emperors. For centuries there were never wanting men like Polycarp and Ignatius, who were ready to die rather than deny

Christ. Fines, and prisons, and torture, and fire, and sword, were unable to crush the spirit of the noble army of martyrs. The whole power of imperial Rome, the mistress of the world, proved unable to stamp out the religion which began with a few fishermen and publicans in Palestine ! And then remember that *believing* was the Church's strength. They won their victory by faith.

Examine the story of the Protestant Reformation. Study the lives of its leading champions—Wycliffe, and Huss, and Luther, and Ridley, and Latimer, and Hooper. Mark how these gallant soldiers of Christ stood firm against a host of adversaries, and were ready to die for their principles. What battles they fought ! What controversies they maintained ! What contradiction they endured ! What tenacity of purpose they exhibited against a world in arms ! And then remember that *believing* was the secret of their strength. They overcame by faith.

Consider the men who have made the greatest marks in Church history in the last hundred years. Observe how men like Wesley, and Whitefield, and Venn, and Romaine, stood alone in their day and generation, and revived English religion in the face of opposition from men high in office—and in the face of slander, ridicule, and persecution from nine-tenths of professing Christians in our land. Observe how men like William Wilberforce, and Havelock, and Hedley Vicars, have witnessed for Christ in the most difficult positions, and displayed a banner for Christ

even at the regimental mess-table, or on the floor of
the House of Commons. Mark how these noble witnesses never flinched to the end, and won the respect
even of their worst adversaries. And then remember
that *believing* is the key to all their characters. By
faith they lived, and walked, and stood, and overcame.

Reader, would you live the life of a Christian
soldier? Pray for faith. It is the gift of God; and
a gift which those who ask shall never ask for in vain.
You must believe before you do. If men do nothing
in religion, it is because they do not believe. Faith
is the first step toward heaven.

Would you fight the fight of a Christian soldier
successfully and prosperously? Pray for a continual
growth of faith. Let your daily prayer be that of
the disciples—"Lord, increase my faith." Watch
jealously over your faith, if you have any. It is the
citadel of the Christian character, on which the safety
of the whole fortress depends. It is the point which
Satan loves to assail. All lies at his mercy if faith is
overthrown. Here, if you love life, you must
especially stand on your guard.

III. The last thing I have to say is this: *True
Christianity is a good fight.*

"Good" is a curious word to apply to any warfare.
All worldly war is more or less evil. No doubt it is
an absolute necessity in many cases, to procure the
liberty of nations, to prevent the weak from being
trampled down by the strong; but still it is an evil.

It entails an awful amount of bloodshed and suffering. It hurries into eternity myriads who are completely unprepared for their change. It calls forth the worst passions of man. It causes enormous waste and destruction of property. It fills peaceful homes with mourning widows and orphans. It spreads far and wide poverty, taxation, and national distress. It disarranges all the order of society. It interrupts the work of the Gospel and the growth of Christian missions. In short, war is an immense and incalculable evil, and every praying man should cry night and day: "Give peace in our times." And yet there is one warfare which is emphatically "good," and one fight in which there is no evil. That warfare is the Christian warfare. That fight is the fight of the soul.

Now what are the reasons why the Christian fight is a "good fight?" What are the points in which his warfare is superior to the warfare of this world? Let me examine this matter, and open it out in order. I dare not pass the subject, and leave it unnoticed. I want no one to begin the life of a Christian soldier without counting the cost. I would not keep back from any one that the Christian fight, though spiritual, is real and severe. It needs courage, boldness, and perseverance. But I want my readers to know that there is abundant encouragement, if they will only begin the battle. The Scripture does not call the Christian fight "a good fight" without reason and cause. Let me try to show what I mean.

(a) The Christian's fight is good *because fought*

under the best of generals. The Leader and Commander of all believers is our Divine Saviour, the Lord Jesus Christ—a Saviour of perfect wisdom, infinite love, and almighty power. The Captain of our salvation never fails to lead His soldiers to victory. He never makes any useless movements, never errs in judgment, never commits any mistake. His eye is on all His followers, from the greatest of them even to the least. The humblest servant in His army is not forgotten. The weakest and most sickly is cared for, remembered, and kept unto salvation. The souls whom He has purchased and redeemed with His own blood are far too precious to be wasted and thrown away. Surely this is good !

(b) The Christian's fight is good, *because fought with the best of helps.* Weak as each believer is in himself, the Holy Spirit dwells in him, and his body is a temple of the Holy Ghost. Chosen by God the Father, washed in the blood of the Son, renewed by the Spirit, he does not go a warfare at his own charges, and is never alone. God the Holy Ghost daily teaches, leads, guides, and directs him. God the Father helps him by His almighty power. God the Son intercedes for him every moment, like Moses on the mount, while he is fighting in the valley below. A threefold cord like this can never be broken ! His daily provisions and supplies never fail. His commissariat is never defective. His bread and his water are sure. Weak as he seems in himself, like a worm, he is strong in the Lord to do great exploits. Surely this is good !

(c) The Christian fight is a good fight, *because fought with the best of promises.* To every believer belong exceeding great and precious promises—all yea and amen in Christ—promises sure to be fulfilled because made by Him who cannot lie, and has power as well as will to keep His word. "Sin shall not have dominion over you." "The God of peace shall bruise Satan under your feet shortly." "He which hath begun a good work in you, will perform it until the day of Jesus Christ." "When thou passest through the waters, I will be with thee; and through the rivers, they shall not overflow thee." My sheep "shall never perish, neither shall any man pluck them out of My hand." "Him that cometh to Me I will in no wise cast out." "I will never leave thee, nor forsake thee." "I am persuaded that neither death, nor life, . . . nor things present, nor things to come, . . . shall be able to separate us from the love of God, which is in Christ Jesus" (Rom. vi. 14; Rom. xvi. 20; Philip. i. 6; Isaiah xliii. 2; John x. 28; John vi. 37; Heb. xiii. 5; Rom. viii. 38, 39). Words like these are worth their weight in gold! Who does not know that promises of coming aid have cheered the defenders of besieged cities like Lucknow, and raised them above their natural strength? Who does not know that the promise of help before night had much to say to the mighty victory of Waterloo? Yet all such promises are as nothing compared to the rich treasure of believers, the eternal promises of God. Surely this is good!

(*d*) The Christian's fight is a good fight, *because fought with the best of issues and results.* No doubt it is a war in which there are tremendous struggles, agonizing conflicts, wounds, bruises, watchings, fastings, and fatigue. But still every believer, without exception, is "more than conqueror through Him that loved him." No soldiers of Christ are ever lost, missing, or left dead on the battle-field. No mourning will ever need to be put on, and no tears be shed for either private or officer in the army of Christ. The muster-roll, when the last evening comes, will be found precisely the same that it was in the morning. The English Guards marched out of London to the Crimean campaign a magnificent body of men; but many of the gallant fellows laid their bones in a foreign grave, and never saw London again. Far different shall be the arrival of the Christian army in " the city which hath foundations, whose builder and maker is God." Not one shall be found lacking. The words of our great Captain shall be found true : "Of them which Thou gavest Me have I lost none" (John xviii. 9). Surely this is good !

(*e*) The Christian's fight is good, *because it does good to the soul of him that fights it.* All other wars have a bad, lowering, and demoralizing tendency. They call forth the worst passions of the human mind. They harden the conscience, and sap the foundations of religion and morality. The Christian warfare alone tends to call forth the best things that are left in man. It promotes humility and charity, it lessens selfishness and worldliness, it induces men to set their affection on things above. The old, the sick, the dying, are never known to repent of fighting Christ's battles against sin, the world, and the devil. Their only regret is that they did not begin to serve Christ long before. The experience of that eminent saint, Philip Henry, does not stand alone. In his last days he said to his family: "I take you all to record that a life spent in the service of Christ is the happiest life that a man can spend upon earth." Surely this is good!

(*f*) The Christian's fight is a good fight, *because it does good to the world.* All other wars have a devastating, ravaging, and injurious effect. The march of an army through a land is an awful scourge to the inhabitants. Wherever it goes it impoverishes, wastes, and does harm. Injury to persons, property, feelings, and morals invariably accompanies it. Far different are the effects produced by Christian soldiers. Wherever they live they are a blessing. They raise the standard of religion and morality. They invariably check the progress of drunkenness, Sabbath-breaking, profligacy, and dishonesty. Even their enemies are obliged to respect them. Go where you please, you will rarely find that barracks and garrisons do good to the neighbourhood. But go where you please, you will find that the presence of a few true Christians is a blessing. Surely this is good!

(*g*) Finally, the Christian's fight is good, *because it*

ends in a glorious reward for all who fight it. Who can tell the wages that Christ will pay to all His faithful people? Who can estimate the good things that our Divine Captain has laid up for those who confess Him before men? A grateful country can give to her successful warriors medals, Victoria crosses, pensions, peerages, honours, and titles. But it can give nothing that will last and endure for ever, nothing than can be carried beyond the grave. Palaces like Blenheim and Strathfieldsay can only be enjoyed for a few years. The bravest generals and soldiers must go down one day before the king of terrors. Better, far better, is the position of him who fights under Christ's banner against sin, the world, and the devil. He may get little praise of man while he lives, and go down to the grave with little honour; but he shall have that which is far better, because far more enduring. He shall have " a crown of glory that fadeth not away." Surely this is good.

Reader, settle it in your mind that the Christian fight is a good fight, really good, truly good, emphatically good. You see only part of it yet. You see the struggle, but not the end; you see the campaign, but not the reward; you see the cross, but not the crown. You see a few humble, broken-spirited, penitent, praying people, enduring hardships and despised by the world; but you see not the hand of God over them, the face of God smiling on them, the kingdom of glory prepared for them. These things are yet to be revealed. Judge not by appearances. There are

more good things about the Christian warfare than
you see.

And now, reader, let me conclude my whole subject
with a few words of practical application. Our lot is
cast in times when the world seems thinking of little
else but battles and fighting. The iron is entering
into the soul of more than one nation, and the mirth
of many a fair district is clean gone. Surely at a
time like this a minister may fairly call on men to
remember the spiritual warfare. Bear with me while
I say a few parting words about the great fight of the
soul.

(1) It may be *you are struggling hard for the
rewards of this world.* Perhaps you are straining
every nerve to obtain money, or place, or power, or
pleasure. Reader, if that be your case, take care.
You are sowing a crop of bitter disappointment.
Unless you mind what you are about your latter end
will be to lie down in sorrow.

Thousands have trodden the path you are pursuing,
and have awoke too late to find it end in misery and
eternal ruin. They have fought hard for wealth, and
honour, and office, and promotion, and turned their
backs on God, and Christ, and heaven, and the world
to come. And what has their end been? Often, far
too often, they have found out that their whole life
has been a grand mistake. They have tasted by bitter
experience the feelings of the dying statesman who
cried aloud in his last hours: "The battle is fought:
the battle is fought: but the victory is not won."

Reader, for your own happiness' sake resolve this day to join the Lord's side. Shake off your past carelessness and unbelief. Come out from the ways of a thoughtless, unreasoning world. Take up the cross, and become a good soldier of Christ. Fight the good fight of faith, that you may be happy as well as safe.

Think what the children of this world will often do for liberty, without any religious principle. Remember how Greeks, and Romans, and Swiss, and Tyrolese, have endured the loss of all things, and even life itself, rather than bend their necks to a foreign yoke. Let their example provoke you to emulation. If men can do so much for a corruptible crown, how much more should you do for one which is incorruptible! Awake to a sense of the misery of being a slave. For life, and happiness, and liberty, arise and fight.

Fear not to begin and enlist under Christ's banner. The great Captain of your salvation rejects none that come to Him. Like David in the cave of Adullam, he is ready to receive all who come to him, however unworthy they may feel themselves. None who repent and believe are too bad to be enrolled in the ranks of Christ's army. All who come to Him by faith are admitted, clothed, armed, trained, and finally led on to complete victory. Reader, fear not to begin this very day. There is yet room for you.

Fear not to go on fighting, if you once enlist. The more thorough and whole-hearted you are as a soldier,

F

the more comfortable will you find your warfare. No doubt you will often meet with trouble, fatigue, and hard fighting, before your warfare is accomplished. But let none of these things move you. Greater is He that is for you than all they that be against you. Everlasting liberty or everlasting captivity are the alternatives before you. Choose liberty, and fight to the last.

(2) Reader, *it may be you know something of the Christian warfare*, and are a tried and proved soldier already. If that be your case, accept a parting word of advice and encouragement from a fellow-soldier. Let me speak to myself as well as to you. Let us stir up our minds by way of remembrance. There are some things which we cannot remember too well.

Let us remember that if we would fight successfully we must put on the whole armour of God, and never lay it aside till we die. Not a single piece of the armour can be dispensed with. The girdle of truth, the breastplate of righteousness, the shield of faith, the sword of the Spirit, the helmet of hope, each and all are needful. Not a single day can we dispense with any part of this armour. Well says an old veteran in Christ's army, who died 200 years ago: "In heaven we shall appear, not in armour, but in robes of glory. But here our arms are to be worn night and day. We must walk, work, sleep in them, or else we are not true soldiers of Christ."—(Gurnall's "Christian Armour").

Let us remember the solemn words of an old

warrior, who went to his rest more than 1800 years
ago: "No man that warreth entangleth himself with
the affairs of this life; that he may please Him who
hath chosen him to be a soldier" (2 Tim. ii. 4). May
we never forget that saying!

Let us remember that some have seemed good
soldiers for a little season, and talked loudly of what
they would do, and yet turned back disgracefully in
the day of battle. Let us never forget Balaam, and
Judas, and Demas, and Lot's wife. Whatever we are,
and however weak, let us be real, genuine, true, and
sincere.

Let us remember that the eye of our loving Saviour
is upon us morning, noon, and night. He will never
suffer us to be tempted above that we are able to
bear. He can be touched with the feeling of our infirmities, for He suffered Himself, being tempted.
He knows what battles and conflicts are, for He Himself was assaulted by the prince of this world. Having
such a High Priest, Jesus the Son of God, let us hold
fast our profession.

Let us remember that thousands of soldiers before
us have fought the same battle that we are fighting,
and come off more than conquerors through Him that
loved them. They overcame by the blood of the
Lamb; and so also may we. Christ's arm is quite as
strong as ever, and Christ's heart is just as loving as
ever. He that saved men and women before us, is one
who never changes. He is able to save to the uttermost both you and me and all who come unto God by

Him. Then let us cast doubts and fears away. Let us follow them who through faith and patience inherit the promises, and are waiting for us to join them.

Finally, let us remember that the time is short, and the coming of the Lord draweth nigh. A few more battles and the last trumpet shall sound, and the Prince of Peace shall come to reign on a renewed earth. A few more struggles and conflicts, and then we shall bid an eternal good-bye to sin and sorrow and death. Then let us fight on to the last, and never surrender. Thus saith the Captain of our salvation: "He that overcometh shall inherit all things; and I will be his God, and he shall be My son" (Rev. xxi. 7).

Let me conclude all with the words of John Bunyan, in one of the most beautiful parts of "Pilgrim's Progress." He is describing the end of one of his best and holiest pilgrims:—

"After this it was noised abroad that Mr. Valiant-for-truth was sent for by a summons, by the same party as the others. And he had this word for a token that the summons was true, 'The pitcher was broken at the fountain' (Eccles. xii. 6). When he understood it, he called for his friends, and told them of it. Then said he: 'I am going to my Father's house; and though with great difficulty I have got hither, yet now I do not repent me of all the troubles I have been at to arrive where I am. My sword I give to him that shall succeed me in my pilgrimage, and my courage and skill to him that can get it. My marks and scars I carry with me, to be a witness for me that

I have fought His battles, who will now be my Rewarder.' When the day that he must go home was come, many accompanied him to the river-side, into which, as he went down, he said, ' O death, where is thy sting?' And as he went down deeper, he cried, ' O grave, where is thy victory?' So he passed over, and all the trumpets sounded for him on the other side."

Reader, may our last end be like this!

―――――

H Y M N.

Thus far the Lord hath led us! in darkness and in day,
Through all the varied stages of the narrow homeward way.
Long since He took that journey, He trod that path alone,
Its trials and its dangers full well Himself hath known.

Thus far the Lord hath led us! The promise has not failed,
The enemy, encountered oft, has never quite prevailed;
The shield of faith has turned aside, or quenched each fiery
          dart,
The Spirit's sword in weakest hands has forced him to depart

Thus far the Lord hath led us! The waters have been high,
But yet in passing through them we felt that He was nigh.
A very present helper in troubles we have found;
His comforts most abounded when our sorrows did abound.

Thus far the Lord hath led us! Our need hath been supplied,
And mercy has encompassed us about on every side,
Still falls the daily manna, the pure rock-fountains flow,
And many flowers of love and hope along the wayside grow.

Thus far the Lord hath led us! and will He now forsake
The feeble ones whom for His own it pleaséd Him to take?
Oh, never, never! Earthly friends may cold and faithless
      prove,
But His is changeless pity and everlasting love.

Calmly we look behind us, on joys and sorrows past,
We know that all is mercy now, and shall be well at last;
Calmly we look before us—we fear no future ill,
Enough for safety and for peace, if *Thou* art with us still.

Yes! "they that know Thy name, Lord, shall put their trust
      in Thee,"
While nothing in themselves but sin and helplessness they see.
The race Thou hast appointed us with patience we can run,
Thou wilt perform unto the end the work Thou hast begun.

JUSTIFIED !

JUSTIFIED!

THE word which forms the title of this paper is one of deep importance in religion. It has within it the foundation of sound soul-saving Christianity. It contains the true secret of inward and spiritual comfort. Happy is the man who can use the language of St. Paul, and say from his heart, "Being justified by faith, I have peace with God through Jesus Christ."

I wish to set before every reader of these pages a few thoughts about justification and peace with God. It is a subject we can never understand too well. Before we leave this world let us take care that we see clearly what it is to be "justified." To die ignorant about this is to be ruined to all eternity. We had better never have been born.

There are four things which I propose to bring before you, in order to throw light on the whole subject.

I. Let me show you the chief privilege of a true Christian: "*He has peace with God.*"

II. Let me show you the fountain from which that privilege flows: "*He is justified.*"

III. Let me show you the rock from which that fountain springs: *"Jesus Christ."*

IV. Let me show you the hand by which the privilege is made our own: *" Faith."*

Upon each of these four points I have something to say. May the Holy Ghost make the whole subject peace-giving to some souls ?

I. First of all, let me show the chief privilege of a true Christian: *He has peace with God.*

When the apostle St. Paul wrote his Epistle to the Romans, he used five words which the wisest of the heathen could never have used. Socrates, and Plato, and Aristotle, and Cicero, and Seneca were wise men. On many subjects they saw more clearly than most people in the present day. They were men of mighty minds, and of a vast range of intellect. But not one of them could have said as the Jewish apostle did, " We have peace with God " (Rom. v. 1).

When St. Paul used these words, he spoke not for himself only, but for all true Christians. Some of them no doubt have a greater sense of this privilege than others. All of them find an evil principle within, warring against their spiritual welfare day by day. All of them find their adversary, the devil, waging an endless battle with their souls. All of them find that they must endure the enmity of the world. But all, notwithstanding, to a greater or less extent, " have peace with God."

This peace with God is a calm, intelligent sense of friendship with the Almighty Lord of heaven and earth. He that has it, feels as if there was no barrier and separation between himself and his holy Maker. He can think of himself as under the eye of an all-seeing Being, and yet not feel afraid. He can believe that this all-seeing Being beholds him, and yet is not displeased.

Such a man can see *death* waiting for him, and yet not be greatly moved. He can look back on the many sins of a misspent life and not feel afraid. He can go down into the cold river—close his eyes on all he has on earth—launch forth into a world unknown, and take up his abode in the silent grave—and yet feel peace. Reader, can you ?

Such a man can look forward to the *resurrection* and the judgment, and yet not be greatly moved. He can see with his mind's eye the great white throne—the assembled world—the open books—the listening angels —the Judge Himself, and yet feel peace. Reader, can you ?

Such a man can think of *eternity*, and yet not be greatly moved. He can imagine a never-ending exist-ence in the presence of God, and of the Lamb—an everlasting Sunday—a perpetual communion, and yet feel peace. Reader, can you ?

I know of no happiness compared to that which this peace affords. A calm sea after a storm—a blue sky after a black thunder-cloud—health after sickness—light after darkness—rest after toil—all, all are beautiful and pleasant things. But none, none of them all can give more than a feeble idea of the comfort which those enjoy who have been brought into the state of peace with God. It is " a peace which passeth all understanding " (Phil. iv. 7).

It is *the want* of this very peace which makes many in the world unhappy. Thousands have everything that is thought able to give pleasure, and yet are never satisfied. Their hearts are always aching. There is a constant sense of emptiness within. And what is the secret of all this ? They have no peace with God.

It is *the desire* of this very peace which makes many a heathen do much in his idolatrous religion. Hundreds have been seen to mortify their bodies, and vex their own flesh in the service of some wretched image which their own hands had made. And why ? Because they hungered after peace with God.

It is *the possession* of this very peace on which the value of a man's religion depends. Without it there may be everything to please the eye, and gratify the ear—forms, ceremonies, services, and sacraments—and yet no good done to the soul. The grand question that should try all is the state of a man's conscience. Is it peace ? *Has he peace with God ?*

This is the very peace about which I address you this day. Have you got it ? Do you feel it ? Is it your own ?

If you have it, you are truly *rich*. You have that which will endure for ever. You have treasure which you will not lose when you die and leave the world. You will carry it with you beyond the grave. You will have it and enjoy it to all eternity. Silver and gold you may have none. The praise of man you may never enjoy. But you have that which is far better than either, if you have peace with God.

If you have it not, you are truly *poor*. You have nothing which will last—nothing which will wear—nothing which you can carry with you when your turn comes to die. Naked you came into this world, and naked in every sense you will go forth. Your body may be carried to the grave with pomp and ceremony. A solemn service may be read over your coffin. A marble monument may be put up in your honour. But after all it will be a pauper's funeral, if you die without peace with God.

Remember my warning. Number up your possessions. Take account of all your property. Consider what you have. You may have youth, and health, and riches, and rank; you may have money, and lands, and houses, and horses, and carriages; you may have honour, love, obedience, troops of friends. It is well. Be thankful for it all. But have you peace? I ask again, Have you peace? Let conscience speak, and give an answer.

II. Let me show you, in the next place, the fountain from which true peace is drawn. *That fountain is justification.*

The peace of the true Christian is not a vague, dreamy feeling, without reason and without foundation. He can show cause for it. He builds upon solid ground. He has peace with God, because he is justified.

Without justification it is impossible to have real peace. Conscience forbids it. Sin is a mountain between a man and God, and must be taken away. The sense of guilt lies heavy on the heart, and must be removed. Unpardoned sin will murder peace. The true Christian knows all this well. His peace arises from a consciousness of his sins being forgiven, and his guilt being put away. His house is not built on sandy ground. His well is not a broken cistern, which can hold no water. He has peace with God, because he is justified.

He is justified, and his sins are *forgiven.* However many, and however great, they are cleansed away, pardoned, and wiped out. They are blotted out of the book of God's remembrance. They are sunk into the depths of the sea. They are cast behind God's back. They are searched for and not found. They are remembered no more. Though they may have been like scarlet, they are become as white as snow; though they may have been red like crimson, they are as wool. And so he has peace.

He is justified and *counted righteous* in God's sight. The Father sees no spot in him, and reckons him innocent. He is clothed in a robe of perfect righteousness, and may sit down by the side of angels without feeling ashamed. The holy law of God, which touches the thoughts and intents of men's hearts, cannot condemn him. The devil, the accuser of the brethren, can lay nothing to his charge, to prevent his full acquittal. And so he has peace.

Is he not naturally a poor, weak, erring, defective *sinner*? He is. None knows that better than he does himself. But notwithstanding this, he is reckoned complete, perfect, and faultless before God, for he is justified.

Is he not naturally a *debtor*? He is. None feels that more deeply than he does himself. He owes ten thousand talents, and has nothing of his own to pay. But his debts are all paid, settled, and crossed out for ever, for he is justified.

Is he not naturally liable to the curse of a *broken law*? He is. None would confess that more readily than he would himself. But the demands of the law have been fully satisfied, the claims of justice have been met to the last tittle, and he is justified.

Does he not naturally deserve *punishment*? He does. None would acknowledge that more fully than he would himself. But the punishment has been borne. The wrath of God against sin has been made manifest. Yet he has escaped, and is justified.

Do you know anything of all this? Are you justified? Do you feel as if you were pardoned, forgiven, and accepted before God? Can you draw near to Him with boldness and say, " Thou art my Father and my Friend, and I am Thy reconciled child?" Oh, believe me, you will never taste true peace until you are justified!

Where are your sins? Are they removed and taken

away from off your soul ? Have they been reckoned for, and accounted for, in God's presence ? Oh, be very sure these questions are of the most solemn importance! A peace of conscience not built on justification is a perilous dream. From such a peace the Lord deliver you !

Go with me in imagination to some of our great London hospitals. Stand with me there by the bedside of some poor creature in the last stage of an incurable disease. He lies quiet perhaps, and makes no struggle. He does not complain of pain perhaps, and does not appear to feel it. He sleeps, and is still. His eyes are closed. His head reclines on his pillow. He smiles faintly, and mutters something. He is dreaming of home, and his mother, and his youth. His thoughts are far away.—But is this health ? Oh, no; no! It is only the effect of opiates. Nothing can be done for him. He is dying daily. The only object is to lessen his pain. His quiet is an unnatural quiet. His sleep is an unhealthy sleep. Reader, you see in that man's case a vivid likeness of *peace without justification.* It is a hollow, deceptive, unhealthy thing. Its end is death.

Go with me in imagination to some lunatic asylum. Let us visit some case of incurable delusion. We shall probably find someone who fancies that he is rich and noble, or a king. See how he will take the straw from off the ground, twist it round his head, and call it a crown. Mark how he will pick up stones and gravel, and call them diamonds and pearls. Hear how he will

laugh, and sing, and appear to be happy in his delusions.
—But is this happiness? Oh, no! We know it is
only the result of ignorant insanity. Reader, you see
in that man's case another likeness of *peace built on
fancy, and not on justification.* It is a senseless,
baseless thing. It has neither root nor life.

Settle it in your mind that there can be no peace
with God, unless we feel that we are justified. *We
must know what is become of our sins.* We must
have a reasonable hope that they are forgiven, and put
away. We must have the witness of our conscience
that we are reckoned not guilty before God. Without
this it is vain to talk of peace. We have nothing but
the shadow and imitation of it. " There is no peace,
saith my God, to the wicked " (Isa. lvii. 21).

Did you ever hear the sound of the trumpets which
are blown before the judges, as they come into the city
to open the assize? Did you ever reflect how different
are the feelings which these trumpets awaken in the
minds of different men? The innocent man, who has
no cause to be tried, hears them unmoved. They
proclaim no terrors to him. He listens and looks on
quietly, and is not afraid. But often there is some
poor wretch waiting his trial in a silent cell, to whom
those trumpets are a knell of despair. They tell him
that the day of trial is at hand. Yet a little time and
he will stand at the bar of justice, and hear witness
after witness telling the story of his misdeeds. Yet a
little time, and all will be over—the trial, the verdict,
and the sentence—and there will remain nothing for

G

him but punishment and disgrace. No wonder the
prisoner's heart beats when he hears that trumpet's
sound !

There is a day fast coming when all who are *not
justified* shall despair in like manner. The voice of the
archangel and the trump of God shall scatter to the
winds the false peace which now buoys up many a soul.
The day of judgment shall convince thousands of self-
willed people, too late, that it needs something more
than a few beautiful ideas about God's love and mercy
to reconcile a man to his Maker, and to deliver his
guilty soul from hell. No hope shall stand in that
awful day but the hope of the justified man. No peace
shall prove solid, substantial, and unbroken, but the
peace which is built on *justification*.

Is this peace your own ? Rest not, rest not, if you
love life, till you know and feel that you are a justified
man. Think not that this is a mere matter of names
and words. Flatter not yourself with the idea that
justification is an " abstruse and difficult subject,"
and that you may get to heaven well enough without
knowing anything about it. Make up your mind to the
great truth that there can be no heaven without peace
with God, and no peace with God without justification.
And then give your soul no rest till you are a justified
man.

III. Let me show you, in the third place, the rock
from which justification and peace with God flow.
That rock is Christ.

The true Christian is not justified because of any goodness of his own. His peace is not to be traced up to any work that he has done. It is not purchased by his prayers and regularity, his repentance and his amendment, his morality and his charity. All these are utterly unable to justify him. In themselves they are defective in many things, and need a large forgiveness. And as to justifying him, such a thing is not to be named. Tried by the perfect standard of God's law the best of Christians is nothing better than a justified sinner, a pardoned criminal. As to merit, worthiness, desert, or claim upon God's mercy, he has none. Peace built on any such foundations as these is utterly worthless. The man who rests upon them is miserably deceived.

Never were truer words put on paper than those which Richard Hooker penned on this subject years ago. Let those who would like to know what English clergymen thought in olden times, mark well what he says: "If God would make us an offer thus large, 'Search all the generation of men since the fall of your father, Adam, and find *one man* that hath done any *one action* which hath past from him pure, without any stain or blemish at all—and for that one man's one only action, neither man nor angel shall find the torments which are prepared for both;' do you think this ransom, to deliver man and angels, would be found among the sons of men? The best things we do have somewhat in them to be pardoned. How then can we do *anything* meritorious and worthy to be rewarded?" To these words I desire entirely to subscribe. I believe that no man can be justified by his works before God in the slightest possible degree. Before man he may be justified. His works may evidence his Christianity. Before God he cannot be justified by anything that he can do. He will be always defective, always imperfect, always shortcoming, always far below the mark, so long as he lives. It is not by works of his own that anyone ever has peace and is a justified man.

But how then is a true Christian justified? What is the secret of that peace and sense of pardon which he enjoys? How can we understand a holy God dealing with a sinful man as with one innocent, and reckoning him righteous notwithstanding his many sins?

The answer to all these questions is short and simple. The true Christian is counted righteous for the sake of a Divine Saviour, Jesus Christ, the Son of God. He is justified because of the death and atonement of Christ. He has peace because Christ died for his sins according to the Scripture. This is the key that unlocks the mighty mystery. Here the great problem is solved, how God can be just and yet justify the ungodly. The life and death of the Lord Jesus explain all. " He is our peace " (Ephes. ii. 14).

Christ has *stood in the place* of the true Christian. He has become his surety and his substitute. He has undertaken to bear all that was to be borne, and to do all that was to be done. Hence the true Christian is a justified man.

Christ has *suffered for sins*, the just for the unjust. He has endured our punishment in His own body on the cross. He has allowed the wrath of God, which we deserved, to fall on His own head. Hence the true Christian is a justified man.

Christ has *paid the debt* the Christian owed, by His own blood. He has reckoned for it, and discharged it to the uttermost farthing by His own precious death. God is a just God, and will not require His debts to be paid twice over. Hence the true Christian is a justified man.

Christ has *obeyed the law* of God perfectly. The prince of this world could find no fault in Him. By so fulfilling it He brought in an everlasting righteousness, in which all His people are clothed in the sight of God. Hence the true Christian is a justified man.

Christ, in one word, has lived for the true Christian. Christ has died for him. Christ has gone to the grave for him. Christ has risen again for him. Christ has ascended up on high for him, and gone into heaven to intercede for his soul. Christ has done all, paid all, suffered all that was needful for his redemption. Hence arises the true Christian's justification—hence his peace. In himself there is nothing, but in Christ he has all things that his soul can require.

Who can tell the blessedness of the exchange that takes place between the true Christian and the Lord Jesus Christ! Christ's righteousness is placed upon him, and his sins are placed upon Christ. Christ has been reckoned a sinner for his sake, and now he is

reckoned innocent for Christ's sake. Christ has been
condemned for his sake, though there was no fault in
Him—and now he is acquitted for Christ's sake, though
he is covered with sins, faults, and shortcomings. Here
is wisdom indeed! God can now be just and yet pardon
the ungodly. Man can feel that he is a prisoner, and
yet have a good hope of heaven and feel peace within.
Who among men could have imagined such a thing?
Who ought not to admire it when he hears it?

We read in British history of a Lord Nithsdale, who
was sentenced to death for a great political crime. He
was closely confined in prison after his trial. The day
of his execution was fixed. There seemed no chance of
escape. And yet before the sentence was carried into
effect he contrived to escape through the skill and
affection of his wife. She brought him a woman's
clothes into the cell where he lay. She disguised him
in them and made him appear like her own maid-
servant. She then went out of the prison with him
following as her attendant, and though he passed
through guards and keepers, none detected him. Who
would not admire the skill and the love of such a wife
as this?

But we read in Gospel history of a display of love,
compared to which the love of Lady Nithsdale is
nothing. We read of Jesus the Son of God coming
down to a world of sinners, who neither cared for Him
before He came, nor honoured Him when He appeared.
We read of Him going down to the prison-house, and
submitting to be bound, that we, the poor prisoners,

might be able to go free. We read of Him becoming
obedient to death—and that the death of the cross—
that we the unworthy children of Adam might have a
door opened to life everlasting. We read of Him being
content to bear our sins and carry our transgressions,
that we might wear His righteousness, and walk in the
light and liberty of the sons of God.

This may well be called a "love that passeth knowledge!" In no way could free grace ever have shown
so brightly as in the way of *justification by Christ*
(Ephes. iii. 19).

This is *the old way* by which alone the children of
Adam, who have been justified from the beginning of
the world, have found their peace. From Abel downwards, no man or woman has ever had one drop of
mercy excepting through Christ. To Him every altar
that was raised before the time of Moses was intended
to point. To Him every sacrifice and ordinance of the
Jewish law was meant to direct the children of Israel.
Of Him all the prophets testified. In a word, if you
lose sight of justification by Christ, a large part of the
Old Testament Scripture will become a tangled maze.

This, above all, is the way of justification which
exactly *meets the wants and requirements of human
nature*. There is a conscience left in man, although
he is a fallen being. There is a dim sense of his own
need, which in his better moments will make itself
heard, and which nothing but Christ can satisfy. So
long as his conscience is not hungry, any religious toy
will satisfy a man's soul and keep him quiet. But once

let his conscience become hungry, and nothing will quiet him but food, and no food but Christ.

There is something within a man, when his conscience is really awake, which whispers, "*there must be a price paid for my soul, or no peace.*" At once the Gospel meets him with Christ. Christ has already paid a ransom for his redemption. Christ has given Himself for him. Christ has redeemed him from the curse of the law, being made a curse for him (Gal. ii. 20; iii. 13).

There is something within a man, when his conscience is really awake, which whispers, "*I must have some righteousness or title to heaven, or no peace.*" At once the Gospel meets him with Christ. He has brought in an everlasting righteousness. He is the end of the law for righteousness. His name is called, The Lord our Righteousness. God has made Him to be sin for us who knew no sin, that we might be made the righteousness of God in Him (2 Cor. v. 21; Rom. x. 4; Jer. xxiii. 6).

There is something within a man, when his conscience is really awake, which whispers, "*there must be punishment and suffering because of my sins, or no peace.*" At once the Gospel meets him with Christ. Christ hath suffered for sin, the just for the unjust, to bring him to God. He bore our sins in His own body on the tree. By His stripes we are healed (1 Peter ii. 24).

There is something within a man, when his conscience is really awake, which whispers, "*I must have a priest for my soul, or no peace.*" At once the Gospel meets him with Christ. Christ is sealed and appointed by

God the Father to be the Mediator between Himself and man. He is the ordained Advocate for sinners. He is the accredited Counsellor and Physician of sick souls. He is the Great High Priest, the Almighty Absolver, the Gracious Confessor of heavy-laden sinners (1 Tim. ii. 5 ; Heb. viii. 1).

This is the one true way of peace—justification by Christ. Beware lest any turn you out of this way and lead you into any of the false doctrines of the Church of Rome. Alas, it is wonderful to see how that unhappy Church has built a house of error hard by the house of truth ! Hold fast the truth of God about justification, and be not deceived. Listen not to anything you may hear about other mediators and helpers to peace. Remember there is no *mediator* but one—Jesus Christ ; no *purgatory* for sinners but one—the blood of Christ ; no *sacrifice* for sin but one—the sacrifice once made on the cross ; no *works* that can merit anything—but the work of Christ ; no *priest* that can truly absolve—but Christ. Stand fast here, and be on your guard. Give not the glory due to Christ to another.

What do you know of Christ ? I doubt not you have heard of Him by the hearing of the ear. You know His name. You are acquainted, perhaps, with the story of His life and death. But what experimental knowledge have you of Him ? What practical use do you make of Him ? What dealings and transactions have there been between your soul and Him ?

Oh, believe me, there is *no peace with God excepting through Christ !* Peace is His peculiar gift. Peace is

that legacy which he alone had power to leave behind
Him when He left the world. All other peace besides
this is a mockery and a delusion. When hunger
can be relieved without food, and thirst quenched
without drink, and weariness removed without rest,
then, and not till then, will men find peace without
Christ.

Is this peace your own ? Bought by Christ with His
own blood, offered by Christ freely to all who are willing
to receive it—is this peace your own ? Oh, rest not :
rest not till you can give a satisfactory answer to my
question—Have you peace ? Are you justified ?

IV. Let me show you, in the last place, *the hand by
which the privilege of peace is received.*

I ask your special attention to this part of our
subject. There is scarcely any point in Christianity so
important as the means by which Christ, justification,
and peace, become the property of a man's soul. Many,
I fear, would go with me so far as I have gone in this
paper, but here would part company. Let us endeavour
to lay hold firmly on the truth.

The means by which a man obtains an interest in
Christ and all His benefits, is *simple faith.* There is
but one thing needful in order to be justified by His
blood, and have peace with God. That one thing is to
believe on Him. This is the peculiar mark of a true
Christian. He believes on the Lord Jesus for His
salvation. " Believe on the Lord Jesus Christ, and thou
shalt be saved." "Whosoever believeth in Him should

not perish, but have everlasting life" (Acts xvi. 31; John iii. 16).

Without this faith it is *impossible to be saved*. A man may be moral, amiable, good-natured, and respectable. But if he does not believe on Christ, he has no pardon, no justification, no title to heaven. " He that believeth not is condemned already." "He that believeth not the Son shall not see life : but the wrath of God abideth on him." " He that believeth not, shall be damned " (John iii. 18, 36 ; Mark xvi. 16).

Beside this faith *nothing whatever is needed for a man's justification*. Beyond doubt, repentance, holiness, love, humility, prayerfulness, will always be seen in the justified man. But they do not in the smallest degree justify him in the sight of God. Nothing joins a man to Christ, nothing justifies, but simple faith. " To him that worketh not, but believeth on Him that justifieth the ungodly, his faith is counted for righteousness." " We conclude that a man is justified by faith without the deeds of the law" (Rom. iv. 5; iii. 28).

Having this faith, a man *is at once completely justified*. His sins are at once removed. His iniquities are at once put away. The very hour that he believes he is reckoned by God entirely pardoned, forgiven, and a righteous man. His justification is not a future privilege, to be obtained after a long time and great pains. It is an immediate present possession. Jesus says, " He that believeth on Me hath everlasting life." Paul says, " By Him all that believeth are justified from all things " (John vi. 47 ; Acts xiii. 39).

I need hardly say that it is of the utmost importance to have clear views about the nature of true saving faith. It is constantly spoken of as the distinguishing characteristic of New Testament Christians. They are called " believers." In the single Gospel of John, " believing " is mentioned eighty or ninety times. There is hardly any subject about which so many mistakes are made. There is none about which mistakes are so injurious to the soul. The darkness of many a sincere inquirer may be traced up to confused views about faith. Let us try to get a distinct idea of its real nature.

True saving faith is *not the possession of everybody*. The opinion that all who are called Christians are, as a matter of course, believers, is a most mischievous delusion. A man may be baptized, like Simon Magus, and yet have no part or lot in Christ. The visible Church contains unbelievers as well as believers. " All men have not faith " (2 Thess. iii. 2).

True saving faith is *not a mere matter of feeling*. A man may have many good feelings and desires in his mind towards Christ, and yet they may all prove as temporary and short-lived as the morning cloud and the early dew. Many are like the stony-ground hearers, and " hear the word with joy." Many will say under momentary excitement, " I will follow Thee whithersoever Thou goest " (Matt. viii. 19).

True saving faith is *not a bare assent of the intellect* to the fact that Christ died for sinners. This is not a whit better than the faith of devils. They know who

Jesus is. They believe, and they do more, they tremble (James ii. 19).

True saving faith is *an act of the whole inner man.* It is an act of the head, heart, and will, all united and combined. It is an act of the soul, in which—seeing his own guilt, danger, and helplessness—and seeing at the same time Christ offering to save him—a man ventures on Christ—flees to Christ—receives Christ as his only hope—and becomes a willing dependent on Him for salvation. It is an act which becomes at once the parent of a habit. He that has it may not always be equally sensible of his own faith, but in the main he lives by faith, and walks by faith.

True faith has *nothing whatever of merit* about it, and in the highest sense cannot be called a work. It is but laying hold of a Saviour's hand, leaning on a husband's arm, and receiving a physician's medicine. It brings with it nothing to Christ but a sinful man's soul. It gives nothing, contributes nothing, pays nothing, performs nothing. It only receives, takes, accepts, grasps, and embraces the glorious gift of justification which Christ bestows, and by renewed daily acts enjoys that gift.

Of all Christian graces, faith is the most important. Of all it is the simplest in reality. Of all it is the most difficult to make men understand in practice. The mistakes into which men fall about it are endless. Some who have no faith never doubt for a moment that they are believers. Others, who have faith, can never be persuaded that they are believers at all. But nearly every mistake about faith may be traced up to the old root of natural pride. Men will persist in sticking to the idea that they are to pay something of their own in order to be saved. As to a faith which consists in receiving only, and paying nothing at all, it seems as if they could not understand it.

Saving faith is the *hand* of the soul. The sinner is like a drowning man at the point of sinking. He sees the Lord Jesus Christ holding out help to him. He *grasps* it and is saved. This is faith.

Saving faith is the *eye* of the soul. The sinner is like the Israelite bitten by the fiery serpent in the wilderness, and at the point of death. The Lord Jesus Christ is offered to him as the brazen serpent, set up for his cure. He *looks* and is healed. This is faith.

Saving faith is the *mouth* of the soul. The sinner is starving for want of food, and sick of a sore disease. The Lord Jesus Christ is set before him as the bread of life, and the universal medicine. He *receives* it, and is made well and strong. This is faith.

Saving faith is the *foot* of the soul. The sinner is pursued by a deadly enemy, and is in fear of being overtaken. The Lord Jesus Christ is put before him as a strong tower, a hiding place, and a refuge. He *runs* into it and is safe. This is faith.

If you love life, cling fast hold to the doctrine of justification by faith. If you love inward peace, let your views of faith be very simple. Honour every part of the Christian religion. Contend to the death for the necessity of holiness. Use diligently and reverently every appointed means of grace; but do not give to these things the office of *justifying* your soul in the slightest degree. If you would have peace, remember that faith alone justifies, and that not as a meritorious work, but as the act that joins the soul to Christ. Believe me, the crown and glory of the Gospel is "justification by faith without the deeds of the law."

No doctrine can be imagined *so beautifully simple* as justification by faith. It is not a dark mysterious truth, intelligible to none but the great, the rich, and the learned. It places eternal life within the reach of the most unlearned, and the poorest in the land. It must be of God.

No doctrine can be imagined *so glorifying to God*. It honours all His attributes, justice, mercy, and holiness. It gives the whole credit of the sinner's salvation to the Saviour He has appointed. It honours the Son, and so honours the Father that sent Him. It gives man no partnership in his redemption, but makes salvation to be wholly of the Lord. It must be of God.

No doctrine can be imagined *so calculated to put man in his right place*. It shows him his own sinfulness, and weakness, and inability to save his soul by his own works. It leaves him without excuse if he is not saved at last. It offers to him peace and pardon without money and without price. It must be of God.

No doctrine can be imagined *so comforting to a broken-hearted and penitent sinner*. It brings to such an one glad tidings. It shows him that there is hope even for him. It tells him though he is a great

sinner, there is ready for him a great Saviour; and
though he cannot justify himself, God can and will
justify him for the sake of Christ. It must be of God.

No doctrine can be imagined *so satisfying to a true
Christian.* It supplies him with a solid ground of
comfort—the finished work of Christ. If anything was
left for the Christian to do, where would his comfort
be ? He would never know that he had done enough,
and was really safe. But the doctrine that Christ
undertakes all, and that we have only to believe and
receive peace, meets every fear. It must be of God.

No doctrine can be imagined *so sanctifying.* It
draws men by the strongest of all cords, the cord of
love. It makes them feel they are debtors, and in
gratitude bound to love much, when much has been
forgiven. Preaching up works never produces such
fruit as preaching them down. Exalting man's goodness and merits never makes men so holy as exalting
Christ. The fiercest lunatics at Paris became gentle,
mild, and obedient, when Abbé Pinel gave them
liberty and hope. The free grace of Christ will produce far greater effects on men's lives than the
sternest commands of law. Surely the doctrine must
be of God.

No doctrine can be imagined *so strengthening to the
hands of a minister.* It enables him to come to the
vilest of men and say, " There is a door of hope even
for you." It enables him to feel, " While life lasts
there are no incurable cases among the souls under my
charge." Many a minister by the use of this doctrine

can say of souls, "I found them in the state of nature. I beheld them pass into the state of grace. I watched them moving into the state of glory." Truly this doctrine must be of God.

No doctrine can be imagined that *wears so well.* It suits men when they first begin, like the Philippian jailer, crying "What shall I do to be saved?" It suits them when they fight in the forefront of the battle. Like the apostle Paul, they say, "The life that I live, I live by the faith of the Son of God." It suits them when they die, as it did Stephen when he cried, "Lord Jesus, receive my spirit." Yes : many an one has opposed the doctrine fiercely while he lived, and yet on his death-bed has gladly embraced justification by faith, and departed saying that "*he trusted in nothing but Christ.*" It must be of God.

Have you this faith? Do you know anything of simple child-like confidence in Jesus? Do you know what it is to rest your soul's hopes wholly on Christ? Oh, remember that where there is no faith, there is no interest in Christ; where there is no interest in Christ, there is no justification; where there is no justification, there can be no peace with God; where there is no peace with God, there is no heaven! And what then? There remains nothing but hell.

And now let me commend the solemn matters we have been considering to your serious and prayerful attention. I invite you to begin by meditating calmly on peace with God—on justification—on Christ—on faith. These are not mere speculative subjects, fit for

H

none but retired students. They lie at the very root of Christianity. They are bound up with life eternal. Bear with me for a few moments, while I add a few words in order to bring them home more closely to your heart and conscience.

1. Let me, then, for one thing, request every reader of this paper *to remember its title.*

Are you justified? Have you peace with God? You have heard of it. You have read of it. You know there is such a thing. You know where it is to be found. But do you possess it yourself? Is it yet your own? Oh, deal honestly with yourself, and do not evade my question! Are you justified? *Have you peace with God?*

I do not ask whether you think it an excellent thing, and hope to procure it at some future time before you die. I want to know about your state now. To-day, while it is called to-day, I ask you to deal honestly with my question. Are you justified? *Have you peace with God?*

May the question ring in your ears, and never leave you till you can give it a satisfactory answer! May the Holy Spirit of God so apply it to your heart that you may be able to say boldly before you die, "Being justified by faith, I have peace with God through Jesus Christ our Lord!"

2. In the next place, let me offer *a solemn warning* to every reader of this paper who knows that he has not peace with God.

You are not justified ! You have not peace ! Consider for a moment how fearfully great is your *danger* ? You and God are not friends. The wrath of God abideth on you. God is angry with you every day. Your ways, your words, your thoughts, your actions, are a continual offence to Him. They are all unpardoned and unforgiven. They cover you from head to foot. They provoke Him every day to cut you off. The sword that the reveller of old saw hanging over his head by a single hair is but a faint emblem of the danger of your soul. There is but a step between you and hell.

You are not justified ! You have not peace ! Consider for a moment how fearfully great is your *folly* ! There sits at the right hand of God a mighty Saviour, able and willing to give you peace, and you do not seek Him. For ten, twenty, thirty, and perhaps forty years He has called to you, and you have refused His counsel. He has cried, " Come to Me," and you have practically replied, " I will not." He has said, "My ways are ways of pleasantness," and you have constantly said, " I like my own sinful ways far better."

And after all, for what have you refused Christ ? For worldly riches, which cannot heal a broken heart ; for worldly business, which you must one day leave ; for worldly pleasures, which do not really satisfy ; for these things, and such as these, you have refused Christ. Is this wisdom, is this fairness, is this kindness to your soul ?

I do beseech you to consider your ways. I mourn over your present condition with especial sorrow. I

grieve to think how many are within a hair's breadth
of some crushing affliction, and yet utterly unprepared
to meet it. Fain would I draw near to everyone, and
cry in his ear, " Seek Christ ! Seek Christ, that you
may have peace within and a present help in trouble."
Fain would I persuade every anxious parent and wife
and child to become acquainted with Him, who is a
brother born for adversity, and the Prince of Peace—
a friend that never fails nor forsakes, and a husband
that never dies.

May God the Spirit apply this warning to some
reader's soul ! May some who began to read this
paper in thoughtlessness find it a word in season, and
be led into the way of peace !

3. Let me, in the next place, offer *an affectionate
entreaty* to all who want peace and know not where to
find it.

You want peace ! Then seek it without delay from
Him who alone is able to give it—Christ Jesus the
Lord. Go to Him in humble prayer, and ask Him to
fulfil His own promises and look graciously on your soul.
Tell Him you have read His compassionate invitation
to the labouring and heavy-laden. Tell Him that this
is the plight of your soul, and implore Him to give you
rest. Do this, and do it without delay.

Seek Christ Himself, and *do not stop short of
personal dealings with Him*. Rest not in regular
attendance on Christ's ordinances. Be not content
with becoming a communicant and receiving the Lord's

Supper. Think not to find solid peace in this way. You must see the King's face, and be touched by the golden sceptre. You must speak to the Physician, and open your whole case to Him. You must be closeted with the Advocate, and keep nothing back from Him. Oh, reader, remember this. Many are shipwrecked just outside the harbour. They stop short in means and ordinances, and never go straight and direct to Christ. " He that drinks of this water shall thirst again." Christ Himself can alone satisfy the soul.

Seek Christ, *and wait for nothing.* Wait not till you feel you have repented enough. Wait not till your knowledge is increased. Wait not till you have been sufficiently humbled because of your sins. Wait not till you have no ravelled tangle of doubts and darkness and unbelief all over your heart. Seek Christ just as you are. You will never be better by keeping away from Him. From the bottom of my heart I subscribe to old Traill's opinion, " *It is impossible that people should believe in Christ too soon.*" Alas! it is not humility, but pride and ignorance that make so many anxious souls hang back from closing with Jesus. They forget that the more sick a man is, the more need he has of the physician. The more bad a man feels his heart, the more readily and speedily ought he to flee to Christ.

Seek Christ, and *do not fancy you must sit still.* Let not Satan tempt you to suppose that you must wait in a state of passive inaction, and not strive to lay hold upon Jesus. How you can lay hold upon Him I do not pretend to explain. But I am certain it is better to struggle towards Christ and strive to lay hold, than to sit still with our arms folded in sin and unbelief. Better perish striving to lay hold on Jesus, than perish in indolence and sin. Well says old Traill, of those who tell us they are anxious but cannot believe in Christ: "This pretence is as inexcusable as if a man wearied with a journey, and not able to go one step further, should argue, '*I am so tired that I am not able to lie down,*' when indeed he can neither stand nor go."

May God the Spirit apply this invitation to some reader's soul! May it be the means of leading some weary soul into the way of peace.

4. Let me, in the next place, offer *some encouragement* to those who have good reason to hope they have peace with God, but are troubled by doubts and fears.

You have doubts and fears! But what do you expect? What would you have? Your soul is married to a body full of weakness, passions, and infirmities. You live in a world that lies in wickedness, a world in which the great majority do not love Christ. You are constantly liable to the temptations of the devil. That busy enemy, if he cannot shut you out of heaven, will try hard to make your journey uncomfortable. Surely these things ought all to be considered.

Believing reader, so far from being surprised that you have doubts and fears, I should suspect the reality of your peace if you had none. I think little of that grace which is accompanied by no inward conflict. There is seldom life in the heart when all is still, quiet, and one way of thinking. Believe me, a true Christian may be known by his *warfare* as well as by his peace. These very doubts and fears which now distress you are tokens of good. They satisfy me that you have really got something which you are afraid to lose.

Believing reader, I advise you to beware that you do not help Satan by becoming an unjust accuser of yourself, and an unbeliever in the reality of God's work of grace. I advise you to pray for more knowledge of your own heart, of the fulness of Jesus, and of the devices of the devil. Let doubts and fears drive you to the throne of grace, stir you up to more prayer, send you more frequently to Christ. But do not let doubts and fears rob you of your peace. Believe me, you must be content to go to heaven as a sinner saved by grace. And you must not be surprised to find daily proof that you really are a sinner so long as you live.

May the Holy Spirit apply this word of encouragement to some reader's soul! May it be the means of establishing the feet of some doubting brother in the way of peace.

5. Let me, in the last place, offer *some counsel* to all who have peace with God, and desire to keep up a lively sense of it.

It must never be forgotten that a believer's sense of his own justification and acceptance with God admits of many degrees and variations. At one time it may be

bright and clear; at another dull and dim. At one
time it may be high and full, like the flood-tide; at
another low, like the ebb. Our justification is a fixed,
changeless, immovable thing. But our *sense* of justification is liable to many changes.

What, then, are the best means of preserving in a
believer's heart the lively sense of justification which is
so precious to the soul that knows it? I offer a few hints
to believers. But such as they are I offer them, though
I lay no claim to infallibility.

To keep up a lively sense of peace, there must be
constant *looking to Jesus.* As the pilot keeps his eye
on the mark by which he steers, so must we keep our
eye on Christ.

There must be constant *communion with Jesus.*
We must use Him daily as our soul's Physician and
High Priest. There must be daily conference, daily
confession, and daily absolution.

There must be constant *watchfulness* against the
enemies of your soul. He that would have peace must
be always prepared for war.

There must be a constant *following after holiness* in
every relation of life—in our tempers, in our tongues,
abroad and at home. A small speck on the lens of a
telescope is enough to prevent our seeing distant
objects clearly. A little dust will soon make a watch
go incorrectly.

There must be a constant *labouring after humility.*
Pride goes before a fall. Self-confidence is often the
mother of sloth, of hurried Bible-reading, and sleepy

prayers. Peter first said he would never forsake his Lord, though all others did; then he slept when he should have prayed; then He denied Him three times, and only found wisdom after bitter weeping.

There must be constant *boldness in confessing* our Lord before men. Them that honour Christ, Christ will honour with much of His company. When the disciples forsook our Lord they were wretched and miserable. When they confessed Him before the Council, they were filled with "joy and the Holy Ghost."

There must be constant *diligence about means of grace, and good works.* Here are the ways in which Jesus loves to walk. No disciple must expect to see much of his Master, who does not delight in public worship, Bible-reading, private prayer, and constant efforts to mend the world.

Lastly, there must be constant *jealousy* over our own souls, and frequent self-examination. We must be careful to distinguish between justification and sanctification. We must beware that we do not make a Christ of holiness.

I lay these hints before you. I might easily add to them. But I am sure they are among the first things to be attended to by believers, if they wish to keep up a lively sense of their own justification and acceptance with God.

Reader, I conclude all by expressing my heart's desire and prayer that you may know what it is to have true peace in your soul.

If you never had peace yet, may it be recorded in the book of God that this year you sought peace in Christ and found it !

If you have tasted peace already, may your sense of peace mightily increase !

The following passage from a direction for the visitation of the sick, composed by Anselm, Archbishop of Canterbury, about the year 1093, will probably be interesting to many readers :—

"Dost thou believe that thou canst not be saved but by the death of Christ ? The sick man answereth, Yes. Then let it be said unto him, Go to then, and whilst thy soul abideth in thee, put all thy confidence in this death alone. Place thy trust in no other thing. Commit thyself wholly to this death. Cover thyself wholly with this alone. Cast thyself wholly on this death. Wrap thyself wholly in this death. And if God would judge thee, say, 'Lord, I place the death of our Lord Jesus Christ between me and Thy judgment ; and otherwise I will not contend with Thee.' And if He shall say unto thee that thou art a sinner, say, 'I place the death of our Lord Jesus Christ between me and my sins.' If He shall say unto thee that thou hast deserved damnation, say, 'Lord, I put the death of our Lord Jesus Christ between Thee and all my sins ; and I offer His merits for my own, which I should have, and have not.' If He say that He is angry with thee, say, 'Lord, I place the death of our Lord Jesus Christ between me and Thy anger.'"—*Quoted by Owen in his Treatise on Justification.*—JOHNSTONE'S EDITION OF OWEN'S WORK. Vol. v. p. 37.

PEACE, perfect peace ? in this dark world of sin !
The blood of Jesus whispers peace within.

Peace, perfect peace ? by thronging duties pressed !
To do the will of Jesus, this is rest.

Peace, perfect peace ? with sorrows surging round !
On Jesus' bosom nought but calm is found.

Peace, perfect peace ? with loved ones far away !
In Jesus' keeping we are safe, and they.

Peace, perfect peace ? our future all unknown !
Jesus we know, and He is on the throne.

Peace, perfect peace ? death shadowing us and ours !
Jesus has vanquished death and all its powers.

It is enough : earth's struggles soon shall cease,
And Jesus call us to heaven's perfect peace.

E. H. Bickersteth.

RICH AND POOR.

RICH AND POOR.

LUKE XVI. 19—23.

" There was a certain rich man, which was clothed in purple and
fine linen, and fared sumptuously every day :

" And there was a certain beggar named Lazarus, which was laid
at his gate, full of sores,

" And desiring to be fed with the crumbs that fell from the rich
man's table : moreover, the dogs came and licked his sores.

" And it came to pass, that the beggar died, and was carried by
the angels into Abraham's bosom : the rich man also died,
and was buried ;

" And in hell he lift up his eyes, being in torments, and seeth
Abraham afar off, and Lazarus in his bosom."

THERE are probably few readers of the Bible who
are not familiar with the parable of the Rich
Man and Lazarus. It is one of those passages of
Scripture which leave an indelible impression on the
mind. Like the parable of the Prodigal Son, once read
it is never forgotten.

The reason of this is clear and simple. The whole
parable is a most vividly painted picture. The story,
as it goes on, carries our senses with it with irresistible

power. Instead of readers, we become lookers on. We are witnesses of all the events described. We see. We hear. We fancy we could almost touch. The rich man's banquet,—the purple,—the fine linen,—the gate,—the beggar lying by it,—the sores,—the dogs,—the crumbs, the two deaths,—the rich man's burial,—the ministering angels,—the bosom of Abraham,—the rich man's fearful waking up,—the fire,—the gulf,—the hopeless remorse, —all, all stand out before our eyes in bold relief, and stamp themselves upon our minds. This is the perfection of language. This is the attainment of the famous Arabian standard, "He speaks the best who turns the ear into an eye."

But after all, it is one thing to admire the masterly composition of this parable, and quite another to receive the spiritual lesson it contains. The eye of the intellect can often see beauties while the heart remains asleep, and sees nothing at all. Hundreds read Pilgrim's Progress with deep interest, to whom the struggle for the celestial city is foolishness. Thousands are familiar with every word of the parable before us this day, who never consider how it comes home to their own case. Their conscience is deaf to the cry which ought to ring in their ears as they read, "Thou art the man." Their heart never turns to God with the solemn inquiry, " Lord, is this my picture ?—Lord, is it I ? "

Reader, I invite you this day to consider the leading truth which this parable is meant to teach us. I purposely omit to notice any part of it but that which stands at the head of this paper. May the Holy Ghost give you a teachable spirit, and an understanding heart, and so produce lasting impressions on your soul!

I. Observe, first of all, *how different are the conditions which God allots to different men.*

The Lord Jesus begins the parable by telling us of a rich man and a beggar. He says not a word in praise either of poverty or of riches. He describes the circumstances of a wealthy man and the circumstances of a poor man; but neither condemns the temporal position of one, nor praises that of the other.

The contrast between the two men is painfully striking. Look on this picture, and on that.

Here is one who possessed abundance of this world's good things. "He was clothed in purple and fine linen, and fared sumptuously every day."

Here is another who has literally nothing. He is a friendless, diseased, half-starved pauper. "He lies at the rich man's gate full of sores," and begs for crumbs.

Both are children of Adam. Both came from the same dust, and belong to one family. Both are living in the same land and subjects of the same government. And yet how different is their condition!

But we must take heed that we do not draw lessons from the parable which it was never meant to teach. The rich are not always bad men, and do not always go to hell: the poor are not always good men, and do not always go to heaven. We must not rush into the extreme of supposing that it is sinful to be rich. We

I

must not run away with the idea that there is anything
wicked in the difference of condition here described,
and that God intended all men to be equal. There is
nothing in our Lord Jesus Christ's words to warrant any
such conclusion. He simply describes things as they
are often seen in the world, and as we must expect to
see them.

Many in every age have disturbed society by stirring
up the poor against the rich. But so long as the world
is under the present order of things universal equality
cannot be attained.

So long as some are wise and some are foolish,—some
strong and some weak,—some healthy and some
diseased;—so long as children reap the fruit of their
parent's misconduct;—so long as sun, and rain, and
heat, and cold, and wind, and waves, and drought, and
blight, and storm, and tempest are beyond man's con-
trol,—so long there will be inequality.

Take all the property in England by force this day,
and divide it equally among the inhabitants. Give
every man above twenty years old an equal portion.
Let all take share and share alike, and begin the world
over again. Do this, and see where you would be at
the end of fifty years. You would just have come round
to the point where you began : you would just find
things as unequal as before. Some would have worked
and some would have been idle : some would have been
always careless and some always scheming; some
would have sold and others would have bought; some
would have wasted and others would have saved. And

the end would be, that some would be rich and others poor.

We might as well say that all men ought to be of the same height, weight, strength, and cleverness,—or that all oak trees ought to be of the same shape and size,—or that all blades of grass ought to be of the same length,—as that all men were meant to be equal.

Settle it in your mind that the main cause of all the suffering you see around you is sin. Sin is the grand cause of the enormous luxury of the rich, and the painful degradation of the poor,—of the heartless selfishness of the highest classes, and the helpless poverty of the lowest. Sin must be first cast out of the world; the hearts of all men must be renewed and sanctified; the devil must be bound; the Prince of Peace must come down and take His great power and reign: all this must be before there ever can be universal happiness, or the gulf be filled up which now divides the rich and poor.

Beware of expecting a millennium to be brought about by any method of government, by any system of education, by any political party. Labour might and main to do good to all men; pity your poorer brethren, and help every reasonable endeavour to raise them from their low estate; slack not your hand from any endeavour to increase knowledge,—to promote morality, —to improve the temporal condition of the poor: but never, never forget that you live in a fallen world, that sin is all around you, and that the devil is abroad. And be very sure that the rich man and Lazarus are emblems of two classes which will always be in the world until the Lord comes.

II.   Observe, in the next place, that *a man's temporal condition is no test to the state of his soul.*

The rich man in the parable appears to have been the world's pattern of a prosperous man.   If the life that now is were all, he seems to have had everything that heart could wish.   We know that he was clothed in purple and fine linen, and fared sumptuously every day : we need not doubt that he had everything else which money could procure.   The wisest of men had good cause for saying, " Money answereth all things;" "The rich hath many friends" (Eccles. x. 19 ; Prov. xiv. 20).

But who that reads the story through can fail to see that in the highest and best sense the rich man was pitiably *poor?*   Take away the good things of this life, and he had nothing left,—nothing after death,—nothing beyond the grave, nothing in the world to come.   With all his riches he had no treasure laid up in heaven. With all his purple and fine linen he had no garment of righteousness.   With all his boon companions he had no Friend and Advocate at God's right hand.   With all his sumptuous fare he had never tasted the bread of life. With all his splendid palace he had no home in the eternal world.   Without God, without Christ, without faith, without grace, without pardon, without holiness, he lives to himself for a few short years, and then goes down hopelessly into the pit.   How hollow and unreal

was all his prosperity! Reader, judge what I say,—
The rich man was very poor.

Lazarus appears to have been one who had literally
nothing in the world. It is hard to conceive a case of
greater misery and destitution than his. He had
neither house, nor money, nor food, nor health, nor, in
all probability, even clothes. His picture is one that
can never be forgotten. He lay at the rich man's gate,
covered with sores; he desired to be fed with the
crumbs that fell from the rich man's table: moreover,
the dogs came and licked his sores. Verily the wise
man might well say, " The poor is hated even of his
neighbour." " The destruction of the poor is their
poverty." (Prov. xiv. 20 ; x. 15).

But who that reads the parable to the end can fail to
see that in the highest sense Lazarus was not poor, but
rich ? He was a child of God. He was an heir of
glory. He possessed durable riches and righteousness.
His name was in the book of life. His place was prepared for him in heaven. He had the best of clothing,
—the righteousness of a Saviour. He had the best of
friends,—God Himself was his portion. He had the
best of food,—he had meat to eat the world knew not
of. And, best of all, he had these things for ever.
They supported him in life: they did not leave him in
the hour of death. They went with him beyond the
grave: they were his to eternity. Surely in this point
of view we may well say, not " poor Lazarus," but " rich
Lazarus."

Reader, you would do well to measure all men by

God's standard,—to measure them not by the amount
of their income, but by the condition of their souls.
When the Lord God looks down from heaven and sees
the children of men, He takes no account of many
things which are highly esteemed by the world. He
looks not at men's money, or lands, or titles. He looks
only at the state of their souls, and reckons them accor-
dingly. Oh, that you would strive to do likewise!
Oh, that you would value grace above titles, or intellect,
or gold! Often, far too often, the only question asked
about a man is, "How much is he worth?" It would
be well for us all to remember that every man is pitiably
poor, until he is rich in faith, and rich toward God.

Wonderful as it may seem to some, all the money in
the world is worthless in God's balances compared to
grace! Hard as the saying may sound, I believe that a
converted beggar is far more important and honourable
in the sight of God than an unconverted king. The
one may glitter like the butterfly in the sun for a little
season, and be admired by an ignorant world; but his
latter end is darkness, and misery for ever. The other
may crawl through the world like a crushed worm, and
be despised by every one who sees him; but his latter
end is a glorious resurrection and a blessed eternity
with Christ. Of him the Lord says, "I know thy
.   .   .   poverty, but thou art rich" (Rev. ii. 9).

King Ahab was ruler over the ten tribes of Israel.
Obadiah was nothing more than a servant in his house-
hold. Yet who can doubt which was most precious in
God's sight, the servant or the king?

Ridley and Latimer were deposed from all their dignities, cast into prison as malefactors, and at length burnt at the stake. Bonner and Gardiner, their persecutors, were raised to the highest pitch of ecclesiastical greatness, enjoyed large incomes, and died unmolested in their beds. Yet who can doubt which of the two parties was on the Lord's side?

Baxter, the famous divine, was persecuted with savage malignity, and condemned to a long imprisonment by a most unjust judgment. Jeffreys, the Lord Chief Justice, was a man of infamous character, without either morality or religion. Baxter was sent to jail and Jeffreys was loaded with honours. Yet who can doubt who was the good man of the two, the Lord Chief Justice or the author of the "Saint's Rest?"

Reader, be very sure that riches and worldly greatness are no certain marks of God's favour. They are often, on the contrary, a snare and hindrance to a man's soul. They make him love the world and forget God. What says Solomon? "Labour not to be rich" (Prov. xxiii. 4). What says St. Paul? "They that *will* be rich, fall into temptation, and a snare, and into many foolish and hurtful lusts, which drown men in destruction and perdition" (1 Tim. vi. 9).

Reader, be no less sure that poverty and trial are no certain proof of God's anger. They are blessings in disguise: they are always sent in love and wisdom. They often serve to wean man from the world: they teach him to set his affections on things above. They often show the sinner his own heart: they often make the saint fruitful in good works. What says the book of Job? "Happy is the man whom God correcteth; therefore despise not thou the chastening of the Almighty" (Job v. 17). What says St. Paul? "Whom the Lord loveth He chasteneth" (Heb. xii. 6).

One great secret of happiness in this life is to be of a patient, contented spirit. Strive daily to realize the truth that this life is not the place of reward. The time of retribution and recompense is yet to come: judge nothing hastily before that time. Remember the words of the wise man: "If thou seest the oppression of the poor, and violent perverting of judgment and justice in a province, marvel not at the matter: for He that is higher than the highest regardeth, and there be higher than they" (Eccles. v. 8). Yes: there is a day of judgment yet to come! That day shall put all in their right places. At last there shall be seen a mighty difference between him that feareth God, and him that feareth Him not. The children of Lazarus and the children of the rich man, shall at length be seen in their true colours, and everyone shall receive according to his works.

III. Observe, in the next place, how *all classes alike come to the grave*.

The rich man in the parable died, and Lazarus died also. Different and divided as they were in their lives, they had both to drink of the same cup at the last. Both went to the house appointed for all living: both went to that place where rich and poor meet together. Dust they were, and unto dust they returned.

This is the lot of all men. It will be our own, unless the Lord shall first return in glory. After all our scheming, and contriving, and planning, and studying, —after all our inventions, and discoveries, and scientific attainments,—there remains one enemy we cannot conquer and disarm, and that is Death. The chapter in Genesis, which records the long lives of Methuselah, and the rest who lived before the flood, winds up the simple story of each by two expressive words, "He died." And now, after 4,800 years, what more can be said of the greatest among ourselves? The histories of Marlborough, and Washington, and Napoleon, and Wellington arrive at the same humbling conclusion. The end of each, after all his greatness, is just this, —"He died."

Death is a mighty leveller. He spares none, he waits for none, and stands on no ceremony. He will not tarry till you are ready. He will not be kept out by moats, and doors, and bars, and bolts. The Englishman boasts that his home is his castle, but, with all his boasting, he cannot exclude death. An Austrian nobleman forbade death and the smallpox to be named in his presence. But named or not named, it matters little : in God's appointed hour death will come.

One man rolls lazily along the road in the easiest and handsomest carriage that money can procure; another toils wearily along the path on foot : yet both are sure to meet at last in the same home.

One man, like Absalom, has fifty servants to wait upon him and do his bidding; another has none to lift a finger to do him a service: but both are travelling to a place where they must lie down alone.

One man is the owner of hundreds of thousands; another has scarce a shilling that he can call his own property: yet neither one nor the other can carry one farthing with him into the unseen world.

One man is the possessor of half a county; another has not so much as a garden of herbs: and yet two paces of the vilest earth will be amply sufficient for either of them at the last.

One man pampers his body with every possible delicacy, and clothes it in the richest and softest apparel; another has scarce enough to eat, and seldom enough to put on: yet both alike are hurrying on to a day when "ashes to ashes, and dust to dust," shall be proclaimed over them; and fifty years hence none shall be able to say, "This was the rich man's bone, and this the bone of the poor."

Reader, I know that these are ancient things. I do not deny it for a moment. I am writing stale old things that all men *know:* but I am also writing things that all men do not *feel.* Oh, no! if they did feel them, they would not speak and act as they do.

You wonder sometimes at the tone and language of ministers of the Gospel. You marvel that we press upon you immediate decision. You think us extreme and extravagant, and ultra in our views, because we urge upon you to close with Christ,—to leave nothing uncertain,—to make sure that you are born again and ready for heaven. You hear, but do not approve. You go away, and say to one another, "The man means well, but he goes too far."

But do you not see that the reality of death is continually forbidding us to use other language? We see him gradually thinning our congregations; we miss face after face in our assemblies : we know not whose turn may come next. We only know as the tree falls there it will lie, and that " after death comes the judgment." We *must* be bold and decided, and uncompromising in our language. We would rather run the risk of offending some than of losing any. We would aim at the standard set up by old Baxter :

> " I'll preach as though I ne'er should preach again,
> And as a dying man to dying men ! "

We would realize the character given by Charles II. of one of his preachers : " That man preaches as though death was behind his back. When I hear him I cannot go to sleep."

Oh, that men would learn to live as those who may one day die ! Truly it is poor work to set our affections on a dying world and its short-lived comforts, and for the sake of an inch of time to lose a glorious immortality ! Here we are toiling, and labouring, and wearying ourselves about trifles, and running to and fro like ants upon a heap ; and yet after a few years we shall all be gone, and another generation will

fill our place.   Live for eternity, reader : seek a portion
that can never be taken from you ; and never forget
John Bunyan's golden rule :—" He that would live well,
let him make his dying day his company-keeper."

IV.   Observe, in the next place, *how precious a
believer's soul is in the sight of God.*

The rich man, in the parable, dies and is buried.
Perhaps he had a splendid funeral,—a funeral proportioned to his expenditure while he was yet alive.
But we hear nothing further of the moment when soul
and body were divided.   The next thing we hear of
is that he is in *hell.*

The poor man, in the parable, dies also.   What
manner of burial he had we know not.   A pauper's
funeral among ourselves is a melancholy business : the
funeral of Lazarus was probably no better.   But this
we do know, that the moment Lazarus dies he is
carried by the angels into Abraham's bosom,—carried
to a place of rest, where all the faithful are waiting
for the resurrection of the just.

Reader, there is something to my mind very striking, very touching, and very comforting in this expression of the parable.   I ask your especial attention
to it.   It throws great light on the relation of all
sinners of mankind who believe in Christ to their
God and Father.   It shows a little of the care bestowed
on the least and lowest of Christ's disciples by the
King of kings.

No man has such friends and attendants as the believer, however little he may think it. Angels rejoice over him in the day that he is born again of the Spirit; angels minister to him all through life; angels encamp around him in the wilderness of this world; angels take charge of his soul in death, and bear it safely home. Yes: vile as he may be in his own eyes, and lowly in his own sight, the very poorest and humblest believer in Jesus is cared for by his Father in heaven with a care that passeth knowledge. The Lord has become his Shepherd, and he can want nothing. Only let a man come unfeignedly to Christ and he shall have all the benefits of a covenant ordered in all things and sure.

Is he laden with many sins? Though they be as scarlet they shall be white as snow.

Is his heart hard and prone to evil? A new heart shall be given to him, and a new spirit put in him.

Is he weak and cowardly? He that enabled Peter to confess Christ before his enemies shall make him bold.

Is he ignorant? He that bore with Thomas' slowness shall bear with him, and guide him into all truth.

Is he alone in his position? He that stood by Paul when all men forsook him shall also stand by his side.

Is he in circumstances of special trial? He that enabled men to be saints in Nero's household shall also enable him to persevere.

The very hairs of his head are all numbered. Nothing can harm him without God's permission. He that hurteth him hurteth the apple of God's eye, and injures a brother and member of Christ Himself.

His trials are all wisely ordered. Satan can only vex him as he did Job, when God permits him. No temptation can happen to him above what he is able to bear. All things are working together for his good.

His steps are all ordered from grace to glory. He is kept on earth till he is ripe for heaven, and not one moment longer. The harvest of the Lord must have its appointed proportion of sun and wind, of cold and heat, of rain and storm ; and then, when the believer's work is done, the angels of God shall come for him as they did for Lazarus, and carry him safe home.

Ah, reader, the men of the world little think whom they are despising when they mock Christ's people ! They are mocking those whom angels are not ashamed to attend upon. They are mocking the brethren and sisters of Christ Himself. Little do they consider that these are they for whose sakes the days of tribulation are shortened : these are they by whose intercession kings reign peacefully. Little do they reck that the prayers of men like Lazarus have more weight in the affairs of nations than hosts of armed men.

Believers in Christ who read these pages, you little know the full extent of your privileges and possessions. Like children at school, you know not half your Father is doing for your welfare. Learn to live by faith more than you have done. Acquaint yourself with the fulness of the treasure laid up for you in Christ even now. This world, no doubt, must always be a place of trial while we are in the body; but still there are comforts provided for the brethren of Lazarus which many never enjoy.

V. Observe, in the last place, *what a dangerous and soul-ruining sin is the sin of selfishness.*

You have the rich man in the parable, in a hopeless state. If there was no other picture of a lost soul in hell in all the Bible you have it here. You meet him in the beginning, clothed in purple and fine linen; you part with him at the last, tormented in the everlasting fire.

And yet there is nothing to show that this man was a murderer, or a thief, or an adulterer, or a liar. There is no reason to say that he was an atheist, or an infidel, or a blasphemer. For anything we know, he attended to all the ordinances of the Jewish religion. But we do know that he was lost for ever.

There is something to my mind very solemn in this thought. Here is a man whose outward life in all probability was correct: at all events we know nothing against him. He dresses richly; but then he had money to spend on his apparel. He gives splendid feasts and entertainments; but then he was wealthy, and could well afford it. We read nothing recorded against him that might not be recorded of hundreds and thousands in the present day who are counted respectable and good sort of people. And yet the end of this man is that he goes to hell. Surely this deserves serious attention.

I believe it is meant to teach us *to beware of living only for ourselves.* It is not enough that we are able to say, " I live correctly. I pay every one his due; I discharge all the relations of life with propriety; I attend to all the outward requirements of Christianity." There remains behind another question, to which the Bible requires an answer. "To whom do you live: to yourself or to Christ? What is the great end, aim, object, and ruling motive in your life?" Let men call the question extreme if they please. For myself, I can find nothing short of this in St. Paul's words, " He died for all, that they which live should not henceforth live unto themselves, but unto Him which died for them, and rose again " (2 Cor. v. 15). And I draw the conclusion that if, like the rich man, we live only to ourselves, we shall ruin our souls.

I believe further that this passage is meant to teach us *the damnable nature of sins of omission.* It does not seem that it was so much the things the rich man did, but the things he left undone, which made him miss heaven. Lazarus was at his gate, and he let him alone. But is not this exactly in keeping with the history of the judgment in the twenty-fifth of St. Matthew? Nothing is said there of the sins of commission of which the lost are guilty. How runs the charge?—"I was an hungred, and ye gave Me no meat: I was thirsty, and ye gave Me no drink: I was a stranger, and ye took Me not in: naked, and ye clothed Me not: sick, and in prison, and ye visited Me not " (Matt. xxv. 42, 43). The charge against them is simply that they did not do certain things. On this their sentence turns. And I draw the conclusion again, that except we take heed, sins of omission may ruin our souls. Truly it was a solemn saying of good Archbishop Usher, on his death-bed: "Lord, forgive me all my sins, but specially my sins of omission."

I believe further, that the passage is meant to teach us that *riches bring special danger with them.* Yes! riches, which the vast majority of men are always seeking after,—riches for which they spend their lives, and of which they make an idol,—riches entail on their possessor immense spiritual peril! The possession of them has a very hardening effect on the soul: they chill; they freeze; they petrify the inward man. They close the eye to the things of faith. They insensibly produce a tendency to forget God.

And does not this stand in perfect harmony with all the language of Scripture on the same subject? What says our Lord? "How hardly shall they that have riches enter into the kingdom of God! It is easier for a camel to go through the eye of a needle, than for a rich man to enter the kingdom of God!" (Mark x. 23, 25). What says St. Paul? "The love of money is the root of all evil; which while some coveted after, they have erred from the faith, and pierced themselves through with many sorrows" (1 Tim. vi. 10). What can be more striking than the fact that the Bible has frequently spoken of money as a most fruitful cause of sin and evil? For money Achan brought defeat on the armies of Israel, and death on himself. For money

K

Balaam sinned against light, and tried to curse God's people. For money Delilah betrayed Samson to the Philistines. For money Gehazi lied to Naaman and Elisha, and became a leper. For money Ananias and Sapphira became the first hypocrites in the early Church, and lost their lives. For money Judas Iscariot sold Christ, and was ruined eternally. Surely these facts speak loudly.

Money, in truth is one of the most *unsatisfying* of possessions. It takes away some cares, no doubt, but it brings with it quite as many cares as it takes away. There is trouble in the getting of it; there is anxiety in the keeping of it; there are temptations in the use of it; there is guilt in the abuse of it; there is sorrow in the losing of it; there is perplexity in the disposing of it. Two-thirds of all the strifes, quarrels, and lawsuits in the world, arise from one simple cause—*money!*

Money most certainly is one of the most *ensnaring and heart-changing* of possessions. It seems desirable at a distance: it often proves a poison when in our hand. No man can possibly tell the effect of money on his soul, if it suddenly fall to his lot to possess it. Many an one did run well as a poor man who forgets God when he is rich.

Reader, I draw the conclusion that those who have money, like the rich man in the parable, ought to take double pains about their souls. They live in a most unhealthy atmosphere: they have double need to be on their guard.

I believe, not least, that the passage is meant to *stir up special carefulness about selfishness in these last days.* You have a special warning in 2 Tim. iii. 1, 2; "In the last days perilous times shall come: for men shall be lovers of their own selves, covetous." I believe we have come to the last days, and that we ought to beware of the sins here mentioned, if we love our souls.

Perhaps we are poor judges of our own times: we are apt to exaggerate and magnify their evils, just because we see and feel them; but after every allowance I doubt whether there ever was more need of warnings against selfishness than in the present day. I am sure there never was a time when all classes in England had so many comforts and so many temporal good things; and yet I believe there is an utter disproportion between men's expenditure on themselves and their outlay on works of charity and works of mercy. I see this in the miserable one guinea subscriptions to which many rich men confine their charity; I see it in the languishing condition of many of our best religious societies, and the painfully slow growth of their annual incomes; I see it in the small number of names which appear in the list of contributions to any good work. There are, I believe, thousands of rich people in this country who literally give away nothing at all. I see it in the notorious fact that few, even of those who give, give anything proportioned to their means. I see all this, and mourn over it. I regard it as the selfishness and covetousness predicted as likely to arise in the last days.

Readers, I know that this is a painful and delicate

subject. But it must not on that account be avoided by the minister of Christ. It is a subject for the times, and it needs pressing home. I desire to speak to myself, and to all who make any profession of religion. Of course I cannot expect worldly and utterly ungodly persons to view this subject in Bible light: to them the Bible is no rule of faith and practice; to quote texts to them would be of little use.

But I do ask all professing Christians to consider well what Scripture says against covetousness and selfishness, and on behalf of liberality in giving money. Is it for nothing that the Lord Jesus spoke the parable of the Rich Fool, and blamed him because he was not "rich towards God?" (Luke xii. 21). Is it for nothing that in the parable of the Sower He mentions the deceitfulness of riches as one reason why the seed of the Word bears no fruit? (Matt. xiii. 22.) Is it for nothing that He says, "Make to yourselves friends of the mammon of unrighteousness?" (Luke xvi. 9.) Is it for nothing that He says, "When thou makest a dinner or a supper, call not thy friends, nor thy brethren, neither thy kinsmen, nor thy rich neighbours; lest they also bid thee again, and a recompense be made thee. But when thou makest a feast, call the poor, the maimed, the lame, the blind: and thou shalt be blessed; for they cannot recompense thee: for thou shalt be recompensed at the resurrection of the just?" (Luke xiv. 12-14.) Is it for nothing that He says, "Sell that ye have, and give alms; provide yourselves bags which wax not old, a treasure in the heavens that faileth not, where no thief approacheth, neither moth corrupteth?" (Luke xii. 33.) Is it for nothing that He says, "It is more blessed to give than to receive?" (Acts xx. 35). Is it for nothing that He warns us against the example of the priest and Levite, who saw the wounded traveller, but passed by on the other side? Is it for nothing that He praises the good Samaritan, who denied himself to show kindness to a stranger? (Luke x. 34.) Is it for nothing that St. Paul classes covetousness with sins of the grossest description, and denounces it as idolatry? (Coloss. iii. 5.) And is there not a striking and painful difference between this language and the habits and feeling of society about money? I appeal to any one who knows the world. Let him judge what I say.

Reader, I only ask you to consider calmly the passages of Scripture to which I have referred. I cannot think they were meant to teach nothing at all. That the habits of the East and our own are different I freely allow; that some of the expressions I have quoted are figurative I freely admit: but still, after all, a principle lies at the bottom of all these expressions. Let us take heed that this principle is not neglected. I wish that many a professing Christian in this day, who perhaps dislikes what I am saying, would try to write a commentary on these expressions, and try to explain to himself what they mean.

To know that alms-giving cannot atone for sin is well. To know that our good works cannot justify us s excellent. To know that we may give all our goods to feed the poor, and build hospitals and cathedrals, without any real charity, is most important. But let us beware lest we go into the other extreme, and because our money cannot save us, give away no money at all.

Has any one money who reads these pages? Then take heed and beware of covetousness. Remember you carry weight in the race towards heaven. All men are naturally in danger of being lost for ever; but you are doubly so because of your possessions. Nothing is said to put out fire so soon as earth thrown upon it: nothing, I am sure, has such a tendency to quench the fire of religion as the possession of money. It was a solemn message which Buchanan, on his death-bed, sent to his old pupil, James I.: "He was going to a place where few kings and great men would come." It is possible, no doubt, for you to be saved as well as others. With God nothing is impossible. Abraham, Job, and David were all rich, and yet saved. But oh, take heed to yourself! Money is a good servant, but a bad master. Let that saying of our Lord's sink down into your heart: "How hardly shall a rich man enter into the kingdom of God." Well said an old divine: "The surface above gold mines is generally very barren." Well might old Latimer begin one of his sermons before Edward VI. by quoting three times over our Lord's words: "Take heed and beware of covetousness," and then saying, "What if I should say nothing else these three or four hours?" There are few prayers in our Litany more wise and more necessary than that petition: "In all time of our *wealth*, good Lord deliver us."

Has any one little or no money who reads these pages ? Then do not envy those who are richer than yourself ? Pray for them. Pity them. Be charitable to their faults. Remember that high places are giddy places, and be not too hasty in your condemnation of their conduct : perhaps if you had their difficulties you would do no better yourself. Beware of the love of money : a man may love money overmuch without having any at all. Beware of the love of self : it may be found in a cottage as well as in a palace. And beware of thinking that poverty alone will save you : if you would sit with Lazarus in glory, you must not only have fellowship with him in suffering, but in grace.

Does any reader desire to know the remedy against that love of self, which ruined the rich man's soul, and cleaves to us all by nature, like our skin ? I tell him plainly there is only one remedy, and I ask him to mark well what that remedy is. It is not the fear of hell. It is not the hope of heaven. It is not any sense of duty. Oh, no! The disease of selfishness is far too deeply rooted to yield to such secondary motives as these. Nothing will ever cure it but an experimental knowledge of Christ's redeeming love. You must know the misery and guilt of your own estate by nature ; you must experience the power of Christ's atoning blood sprinkled upon your conscience, and making you whole ; you must taste the sweetness of peace with God through the mediation of Jesus, and feel the love of a reconciled Father shed abroad in your heart by the Holy Ghost.

Then, and not till then, the mainspring of selfishness

will be broken. *Then,* knowing the immensity of your
debt to Christ, you will feel that nothing is too great
and too costly to give to Him. Feeling that you have
been loved much when you deserved nothing, you will
heartily love in return, and cry, " What shall I render
unto the Lord for all His benefits ? " Feeling that you
have freely received countless mercies, you will think it
a privilege to do anything to please Him to Whom you
owe all. Feeling that you have been bought with a
price, and are no longer your own, you will labour to
glorify God with body and spirit, which are His.

Yes, reader, I repeat it this day! I know no *effectual*
remedy for the love of self but a believing apprehen-
sion of the love of Christ. Other remedies may palliate
the disease : this alone will heal it. Other antidotes may
hide its deformity : this alone will work a perfect cure.

An easy, good-natured temper may cover over selfishness in one man ; a love of praise may conceal it in a
second ; a self-righteous asceticism and an affected
spirit of self-denial may keep it out of sight in a third ;
but nothing will ever cut up selfishness by the roots
but the love of Christ revealed in the mind by the
Holy Ghost, and felt in the heart by simple faith.
Once let a man see the full meaning of the words,
" Christ loved me and gave Himself for me," and then
he will delight to give himself to Christ, and all that he
has to His service. He will live to Him, not in order
that he may be secure, but because he is secure already.
He will work for Him, not that he may have life and
peace, but because life and peace are his already.

Go to the cross of Christ, all you that want to be delivered from the power of selfishness. Go and see what a price was paid there to provide a ransom for your soul. Go and see what an astounding sacrifice was there made that a door to eternal life might be provided for poor sinners like you. Go and see how the Son of God gave Himself for you, and learn to think it a small thing to give yourself to Him.

Reader, the disease which ruined the rich man in the parable may be cured. But oh, remember, there is only one real remedy! If you would not live to yourself, you must live to Christ. See to it that this remedy is not only known, but applied,—not only heard of, but used.

1. And now let me conclude all *by urging on every reader of these pages the great duty of self-inquiry.*

A passage of Scripture like this parable ought surely to raise in many an one great searchings of heart. "What am I? Where am I going? What am I doing? What is likely to be my condition after death? Am I prepared to leave the world? Have I any home to look forward to in the world to come. Have I put off the old man and put on the new? Am I really one with Christ, and a pardoned soul?" Surely such questions as these may well be asked when the story of the rich man and Lazarus has been heard. Oh, that the Holy Ghost may incline many a reader's heart to ask them!

2. In the next place, I *invite* all readers who desire to have their souls saved, and have no good account to give of themselves at present, to seek salvation while it can be found. I do entreat you to apply to Him, by Whom alone man can enter heaven and be saved,—even Jesus Christ the Lord. He has the keys of heaven. He is sealed and appointed by God the Father to be the Saviour of all that will come to Him. Go to Him in earnest and hearty prayer, and tell Him your case. Tell Him that you have heard that He receiveth sinners, and that you come to Him as such; tell Him that you desire to be saved by Him in His Own way, and ask Him to save you. Oh that you may take this course without delay! Remember the hopeless end of the rich man. Once dead there is no more change.

3. Last of all, I *entreat* all professing Christians to encourage themselves in habits of liberality towards all causes of charity and mercy. Remember that you are God's stewards, and give money liberally, freely, and without grudging, whenever you have an opportunity. You cannot keep your money for ever. You must give account one day of the manner in which it has been expended. Oh, lay it out with an eye to eternity, while you can!

I do not ask rich men to leave their situations in life and go into the workhouse. I ask no man to neglect his worldly calling, and to omit to provide for his family. Diligence in business is a positive Christian duty: provision for those dependent on us is proper

Christian prudence. But I ask all to look around continually as they journey on, and to remember the poor, —the poor in body and the poor in soul. Here we are for a few short years. How can we do most good with our money while we are here? How can we so spend it as to leave the world somewhat happier and somewhat holier when we are removed? Might we not abridge some of our luxuries? Might we not lay out less upon ourselves, and give more to Christ's cause and Christ's poor? Is there none we can do good to? Are there no sick, no poor, no needy, whose sorrows we might lessen, and whose comforts we might increase? Such questions will never fail to elicit an answer from some quarter. I am thoroughly persuaded that the income of every religious and charitable society in England might easily be multiplied tenfold, if English Christians would give in proportion to their means.

There are none, surely, to whom such appeals ought to come home with such power as professing believers in the Lord Jesus. The parable of the text is a striking illustration of our position by nature, and our debt to Christ. We all lay, like Lazarus at heaven's gate, sick unto the death, helpless, and starving. Blessed be God, we were not neglected as he was! Jesus came forth to relieve us. Jesus gave Himself for us, that we might have hope and live. For a poor Lazarus-like world He came down from heaven, and humbled Himself to become a man. For a poor Lazarus-like world He went up and down doing good, caring for men's bodies as well as souls, until He died for us on the cross.

I believe that in giving to support works of charity and mercy we are doing that which is according to Christ's mind,—and I ask readers of these pages to begin the habit of giving, if they never began it before; and to go on with it increasingly, if they have begun.

I believe that in offering a warning against covetousness I have done no more than bring forward a warning specially called for by the times, and I ask God to bless the consideration of these pages to many souls.

THE MORNING WITHOUT CLOUDS.

THE MORNING WITHOUT CLOUDS.

"He shall be as the light of the morning, when the sun riseth, even a morning without clouds ; as the tender grass springing out of the earth by clear shining after rain. Although my house be not so with God ; yet He hath made with me an everlasting covenant, ordered in all things, and sure : for this is all my salvation, and all my desire, although He make it not to grow."—2 SAM. xxiii. 4, 5.

THE text which heads this page is taken from a chapter which ought to be very interesting to every Christian. It begins with the touching expression, "These be the last words of David."

Whether that means, "these are the last words which David ever spoke by inspiration as a Psalmist," or "these are among the last sayings of David before his death," signifies little. In either point of view, the phrase suggests many thoughts.

It contains the experience of an old servant of God who had many ups and downs in his life. It is the old soldier remembering his campaigns. It is the old traveller looking back on his journeys.

I. Let us first consider *David's humbling confession.*

He looks forward with a prophetic eye to the

future coming of the Messiah, the promised Saviour, the seed of Abraham, and the seed of David. He looks forward to the advent of a glorious kingdom in which there shall be no wickedness, and righteousness shall be the universal character of all the subjects. He looks forward to the final gathering of a perfect family in which there shall be no unsound members, no defects, no sin, no sorrow, no deaths, no tears. And he says, the light of that kingdom shall be " as the light of the morning when the sun riseth, even a morning without clouds."

But then he turns to his own family, and sorrowfully says, " My house is not so with God." It is not perfect, it is not free from sin, and it has blots and blemishes of many kinds. It has cost me many tears. It is not so as I could wish, and so as I have vainly tried to make it.

Poor David might well say this! If ever there was a man whose house was full of trials, and whose life was full of sorrows, that man was David. Trials from the envy of his own brethren,—trials from the unjust persecution of Saul,—trials from his own servants, such as Joab and Ahithophel,—trials from a wife, even that Michal who once loved him so much,—trials from his children, such as Absalom, Amnon, and Adonijah,—trials from his own subjects, who at one time forgot all he had done, and drove him out of Jerusalem by rebellion,—trials of all kinds, wave upon wave, were continually breaking on David to the very end of his days. Some of the worst of these trials, no doubt, were the just consequences of his own sins, and the wise chastisement of a loving Father. But we must have hard hearts if we do not feel that David was indeed " a man of sorrows."

But is not this the experience of many of God's noblest saints and dearest children ? What careful reader of the Bible can fail to see that Adam, and Noah, and Abraham, and Isaac, and Jacob, and Joseph, and Moses, and Samuel were all men of many sorrows, and that those sorrows chiefly arose out of their own homes ?

The plain truth is that home trials are one of the many means by which God sanctifies and purifies His believing people. By them He keeps us humble. By them He draws us to Himself. By them He sends us to our Bibles. By them He teaches us to pray. By them He shows us our need of Christ. By them He weans us from the world. By them He prepares us for " a city which hath foundations," in which there will be no disappointments, no tears, and no sin. It is no special mark of God's favour when Christians have no trials. They are spiritual medicines, which poor fallen human nature absolutely needs. King Solomon's course was one of unbroken peace and prosperity. But it may well be doubted whether this was good for his soul.

Before we leave this part of our subject, let us learn some practical lessons.

(a) Let us learn that *parents cannot give grace*

L

to their children, or masters to their servants. We may use all means, but we cannot command success. We may teach, but we cannot convert. We may show those around us the bread and water of life, but we cannot make them eat and drink it. We may point out the way to eternal life, but we cannot make others walk in it. "It is the Spirit that quickeneth." Life is that one thing which the cleverest man of science cannot create or impart. It comes "not of blood, nor of the will of man" (John i. 13). To give life is the grand prerogative of God.

(*b*) Let us learn *not to expect too much* from anybody or anything in this fallen world. One great secret of unhappiness is the habit of indulging in exaggerated expectations. From money, from marriage, from business, from houses, from children, from worldly honours, from political success, men are constantly expecting what they never find; and the great majority die disappointed. Happy is he who has learned to say at all times, "My soul, wait thou only upon God; my expectation is from Him" (Psalm lxii. 5).

(*c*) Let us learn *not to be surprised* or fret when trials come. It is a wise saying of Job, "Man is born to trouble as the sparks fly upward" (Job v. 7) Some, no doubt, have a larger cup of sorrows to drink than others. But few live long without troubles or cares of some kind. The greater our affections the deeper are our afflictions, and the more we love the more we have to weep. The only certain thing to be predicted about the babe lying in his cradle is this—if he grows up he will have many troubles, and at last he will die.

(d) Let us learn, lastly, that *God knows far better than we do what is the best time* for taking away from us those whom we love. The deaths of some of David's children were painfully remarkable, both as to age, manner, and circumstances. When David's little infant lay sick, David thought he would have liked the child to live, and he fasted and mourned till all was over. Yet, when the last breath was drawn, he said, with strong assurance of seeing the child again, " I shall go to him, but he shall not return to me " (2 Samuel xii. 23). But when, on the contrary, Absalom died in battle— Absalom the beautiful—Absalom the darling of his heart—but Absalom who died in open sin against God and his father, what did David say then ? Hear his hopeless cry, " O Absalom, my son, my son, would God I had died for thee ! " (2 Samuel xviii. 33). Alas ! we none of us know when it is best for ourselves, our children, and our friends to die. We should pray to be able to say, " My times are in Thy hands," let it be when Thou wilt, where Thou wilt, and how Thou wilt (Psalm xxxi. 15).

II. Let us consider, secondly, what was the *source of David's present comfort in life*. He says, "Though my house is not as I could wish, and is the cause of much sorrow, God has made with me an everlasting covenant, ordered in all things, and sure." And then he adds, " this is all my salvation, and all my desire."

Now this word " covenant " is a deep and mysterious thing, when applied to anything that God does. We can understand what a covenant is between man and man. It is an agreement between two persons, by which they bind themselves to fulfil certain conditions and do certain things. But who can fully understand a covenant made by the Eternal God ? It is something far above us and out of sight. It is a phrase by which He is graciously pleased to accommodate Himself to our poor, weak faculties, but at the best we can only grasp a little of it.

The covenant of God to which David refers as his comfort must mean that everlasting agreement or counsel between the Three Persons of the Blessed Trinity which has existed from all eternity for the benefit of all the living members of Christ.

It is a mysterious and ineffable arrangement whereby all things necessary for the salvation of our souls, our present peace, and our final glory, are fully and completely provided, and all this by the joint work of God the Father, God the Son, and God the Holy Ghost. The redeeming work of God the Son by dying as our Substitute on the cross—the drawing work of God the Father by choosing and drawing us to the Son—and the sanctifying work of the Holy Ghost in awakening, quickening, and renewing our fallen nature—are all contained in this covenant, besides everything that the soul of the believer needs between grace and glory.

Of this covenant, the Second Person of the Trinity is the Mediator (Heb. xii. 24). Through Him all the blessings and privileges of the covenant are conveyed to every one of His believing members. And when the Bible speaks of God making a covenant with man, as in the words of David, it means with man in Christ as a member and part of the Son. They are His mystical body, and He is their Head, and through the Head all the blessings of the eternal covenant are conveyed to the body. Christ, in one word, is the Surety of the covenant, and through Him believers receive its benefits. This is the great covenant which David had in view.

True Christians would do well to think about this covenant, remember it, and roll the burden of their souls upon it far more than they do. There is unspeakable consolation in the thought that the salvation of our souls has been provided for from all eternity, and is not a mere affair of yesterday. Our names have long been in the Lamb's book of life. Our pardon and peace of conscience through Christ's blood, our strength for duty, our comfort in trial, our power to fight Christ's battles, were all arranged for us from endless ages, and long before we were born. Here upon earth we pray, and read, and fight, and struggle and groan, and weep, and are often sore let and hindered in our journey. But we ought to remember that an Almighty eye has long been upon us, and that we have been the subjects of Divine provision though we knew it not.

Above all, Christians should never forget that the everlasting covenant is " ordered in all things and sure." The least things in our daily life are working together for good, though we may not see it at the time. The very hairs of our head are all numbered, and not a sparrow falls to the ground without our Father. There is no luck or chance in anything that happens to us. The least events in our life are parts of an everlasting scheme or plan in which God has foreseen and arranged everything for the good of our souls.

Let us all try to cultivate the habit of remembering the everlasting covenant. It is a doctrine full of strong consolation, if it is properly used. It was not meant to destroy our responsibility. It is widely different from Mahommedan fatalism. It is specially intended to be a refreshing cordial for practical use in a world full of sorrow and trial. We ought to remember, amid the many sorrows and disappointments of life, that " what we know not now, we shall know hereafter." There is a meaning, and a " needs be " in every bitter cup that we have to drink, and a wise cause for every loss and bereavement under which we mourn.

After all, how little we know ? We are like children who look at a half-finished building, and have not the least idea what it will look like when it is completed. They see masses of stone, and brick, and rubbish, and timber, and mortar, and scaffolding, and dirt, and all in apparent confusion. But the architect who designed the building sees order in all, and quietly looks forward with joy to the day when the whole building will be finished, and the scaffolding removed and taken away. It is even so with us. We cannot grasp the meaning of many a providence in our lives, and are tempted to think that all around us is confusion. But we should try to remember that the great Architect in heaven is always doing wisely and well, and that we are always being "led by the right way to a city of habitation" (Ps. cvii. 7). The resurrection morning will explain all. It is a quaint but wise saying of an old divine, that "true faith has bright eyes, and can see even in the dark."

It is recorded of Barnard Gilpin, a Reformer who lived in the days of the Marian martyrdoms, and was called the Apostle of the North, that he was famous for never murmuring or complaining whatever happened to him. In the worst and blackest times he used to be always saying, "It is all in God's everlasting covenant, and must be for good." Towards the close of Queen Mary's reign he was suddenly summoned to come up from Durham to London, to be tried for heresy, and in all probability, like Ridley and Latimer, to be burned. The good man quietly obeyed the summons, and said to his mourning friends, "It is all in the covenant, and must be for good." On his journey from Durham to London his horse fell, and his leg was broken, and he was laid up at a roadside inn. Once more he was asked, "What do you think of this?" Again he replied, "It is all in the covenant, and must be for good." And so it turned out. Weeks and weeks passed away before his leg was healed, and he was able to resume his journey. But during those weeks the unhappy Queen Mary died, the persecutions were stopped, and the worthy old Reformer returned to his northern home rejoicing. "Did I not tell you," he said to his friends, "that all was working together for good?"

Well would it be for us if we had something of Barnard Gilpin's faith, and could make practical use of the everlasting covenant as he did. Happy is the Christian who can say from his heart these words,—

> "I know not the way I am going,
>   But well do I know my Guide;
> With a childlike trust I give my hand
>   To the mighty Friend by my side.
> The only thing that I say to Him,
>   As He takes it, is—'Hold it fast;
> Suffer me not to lose my way,
>   And bring me home at last.'"

III. Let us consider, lastly, *what was king David's hope for the future.* That hope, beyond doubt, was the glorious advent of the Messiah at the end of the world, and the setting up of a kingdom of righteousness at the final restitution of all things.

Of course king David's views of this kingdom were dim and vague compared to those which are within reach of every intelligent reader of the New Testament. He was not ignorant of the coming of Messiah to suffer, for he speaks of it in the twenty-second Psalm. But he saw far behind it the coming of Messiah to reign, and his eager faith overleaped the interval between the two Advents. That his mind was fixed upon the promise, that the "seed of the woman should" one day completely "bruise the serpent's head," and that the curse should be taken off the earth, and the effects of Adam's fall completely removed, I feel no doubt at all. The Church of Christ would have done well if she had walked in David's steps, and given as much attention to the Second Advent as David did.

The figures and comparisons which David uses in speaking of the advent and future kingdom of the Messiah are singularly beautiful, and admirably fitted to exhibit the benefits which it will bring to the Church and the earth. The Second Advent of Christ shall be "as the light of the morning when the sun riseth, even a morning without clouds; as the tender grass springing out of the earth by clear shining after rain." Those words deserve a thousand thoughts. Who can look around him, and consider the state of the world in which we live, and not be obliged to confess that clouds and darkness are now on every side? "The whole creation groaneth and travaileth in pain" (Rom. viii. 22). Look where we will we see confusion, quarrels, wars between nations, helplessness of statesmen, discontent and grumbling of the lower classes, excessive luxury among the rich, extreme poverty among the poor, intemperance, impurity, dishonesty, swindling, lying, cheating, covetousness, heathenism, superstition, formality among Christians, decay of vital religion—these are the things which we see continually over the whole globe, in Europe, Asia, Africa, and America. These are the things which defile the face of creation, and prove that the devil is " the prince of this world," and the kingdom of God is not yet come. These are clouds indeed, which often hide the sun from our eyes.

But there is a good time coming, which David saw far distant, when this state of things shall be completely changed. There is a kingdom coming, in which holiness shall be the rule, and sin shall have no place at all.

Who can look around him in his own neighbourhood, and fail to see within a mile of his own house that the consequences of sin lie heavily on earth, and that sorrow and trouble abound? Sickness, and pain, and death come to all classes, and spare none, neither rich or poor. The young often die before the old, and the children before the parents. Bodily suffering of the most fearful description, and incurable disease, make the existence of many miserable. Widowhood, and childlessness, and solitariness, tempt many to feel weary of life, though everything which money can obtain is within their reach. Family quarrels, and envies, and jealousies break up the peace of many a household, and are a worm at the root of many a rich man's happiness. Who can deny that all these things are to be seen on every side of us ? There are many clouds now.

Will nothing end this state of things ? Is creation to go on groaning and travailing for ever after this fashion ? Thanks be to God, the Second Advent of Christ supplies an answer to these questions. The Lord Jesus Christ has not yet finished His work on behalf of man. He will come again one day (and perhaps very soon) to set up a glorious kingdom, in which the consequences of sin shall have no place at all. It is a kingdom in which there shall be no pain and no disease, in which "the inhabitant shall no more say, I am sick" (Isaiah xxxiii. 24). It is a kingdom in which there shall be no partings, no moves, no changes, and no good-byes. It is a kingdom in which there shall be no deaths, no funerals, no tears, and no mourning worn. It is a kingdom in which there shall be no quarrels, no losses, no crosses, no disappointments, no wicked children, no bad servants, no faithless friends. When the last trumpet shall sound, and the dead shall be raised incorruptible, there will be a grand gathering together of all God's people, and when we awake up after our Lord's likeness we shall be satisfied (Psalm xvii. 15). Where is the Christian heart that does not long for this state of things to begin ? Well

may we take up the last prayer in the Book of
Revelation, and often cry, "Come quickly, Lord
Jesus."

(a) And now, have we troubles ?   Where is the
man or woman on earth who can say, "I have none."
Let us take them all to the Lord Jesus Christ.
None can comfort like Him.   He Who died on the
cross to purchase forgiveness for our sins, is sitting
at the right hand of God, with a heart full of love
and sympathy.   He knows what sorrow is, for He
lived thirty-three years in this sinful world, and
suffered Himself being tempted, and saw suffering
every day.   And He has not forgotten it.   When
He ascended into heaven, to sit at the right hand of
the Father, He took a perfect human heart with
Him.   He can be "touched with the feeling of our
infirmities" (Heb. iv. 15).   He can feel.   Almost
His last thought upon the cross was for His Own
mother, and He cares for weeping and bereaved
mothers still.

He would have us never forget that our departed
friends in Christ are not lost, but only gone before.
We shall see them again in the day of gathering
together, for them that "sleep in Jesus will God
bring with Him" (1 Thess. iv. 14).   We shall see
them in renewed bodies, and know them again, but
better, more beautiful, more happy than we ever
saw them on earth.   Best of all, we shall see them
with the comfortable feeling that we meet to part
no more.

(*b*) Have we troubles? *Let us never forget the everlasting covenant* to which old David clung to the end of his days. It is still in full force. It is not cancelled. It is the property of every believer in Jesus, whether rich or poor, just as much as it was the property of the son of Jesse. Let us never give way to a fretting, murmuring, complaining spirit. Let us firmly believe at the worst of times that every step in our lives is ordered by the Lord, with perfect wisdom and perfect love, and that we shall see it all at last. Let us not doubt that He is always doing all things well. He is good in giving, and equally good in taking away.

(*c*) Finally, have we troubles? Let us never forget that *one of the best of remedies and most soothing medicines is to try to do good to others,* and to be useful. Let us lay ourselves out to make the sorrow less and the joy greater in this sin-burdened world. There is always some good to be done within a few yards of our own doors. Let every Christian strive to do it, and to relieve either bodies or minds.

> " To comfort and to bless,
>   To find a balm for woe,
>   To tend the lone and fatherless,
>   Is angel's work below."

Selfish feeding on our own troubles, and lazy poring over our sorrows, are one secret of the melancholy misery in which many spend their lives. If we trust in Jesus Christ's blood, let us remember His example. He ever "went about doing good" (Acts x. 38). He came not to be ministered unto, but to minister, as well as to give His life a ransom for many. Let us try to be like Him. Let us walk in the steps of the good Samaritan, and give help wherever help is really needed. Even a kind word spoken in season is often a mighty blessing. That Old Testament promise is not yet worn out: "Blessed is the man that provideth for the sick and needy; the Lord shall deliver him in the time of trouble" (Psalm xli. 1, Prayer-book version).

FAITH'S CHOICE.

FAITH'S CHOICE.

HEBREWS XI. 24—26.

"By faith Moses, when he was come to years, refused to be
called the son of Pharaoh's daughter;
"Choosing rather to suffer affliction with the people of God,
than to enjoy the pleasures of sin for a season;
"Esteeming the reproach of Christ greater riches than the
treasures in Egypt: for he had respect unto the recompense
of the reward."

THE eleventh chapter of the Epistle to the
Hebrews is a great chapter I need not tell you.
I can well believe it must have been most
cheering and encouraging to a converted Jew. I
suppose none found so much difficulty in a profession
of Christianity as the Hebrews did. The way was
narrow to all, but pre-eminently so to them. The
cross was heavy to all, but surely they had to carry
double weight. And this chapter would refresh them
like a cordial,—it would be as "wine to those of a
heavy heart." Its words would be pleasant as the
honey-comb, "sweet to the soul, and health to the
bones."

The three verses I am going to explain are far from
being the least interesting in the chapter. Indeed I
think few, if any, have so strong a claim on our
attention. And I will tell you why I say so.

M

It seems to me that the work of faith here spoken of, comes home more especially to our own case. The men of God who are named in the former part of the chapter are all examples to us, beyond question. But we cannot literally do what most of them did, however much we may drink into their spirit. We are not called upon to offer a literal sacrifice like Abel—or build a literal ark like Noah—or leave our country literally, and dwell in tents, and offer up our Isaac like Abraham. But the faith of Moses comes nearer to us. It seems to operate in a way more familiar to our own experience. It made him take up a line of conduct such as we must often take up ourselves in the present day, each in our own walk of life. And for this reason I think these three verses deserve more than ordinary consideration.

Now I have nothing but the simplest things to say about them. I shall only try to enforce upon you the greatness of the things Moses did, and the principle on which he did them. And then perhaps you will be better prepared for the practical instruction which the verses appear to hold out to every one who will receive it.

May the Holy Ghost bless the subject to us all! May He give us the same spirit of faith, that we may walk in the steps of Moses, do as he did, and share his reward!

I. First, then, I will speak of *what Moses gave up and refused.*

Moses gave up three things for the sake of his soul.

He felt that his soul would not be saved if he kept them, so he gave them up.   And in so doing, I say that he made three of the greatest sacrifices that man's heart can make.

1. *He gave up rank and greatness.*

" He refused to be called the son of Pharaoh's daughter." You all know his history. The daughter of Pharaoh had preserved his life, when he was an infant—adopted him and educated him as her own son.

If writers of history may be trusted, she was Pharaoh's only child. Men go so far as to say that in the common order of things Moses would one day have been king of Egypt. That may be, or may not—we cannot tell. It is enough for us to know that, from his connection with Pharaoh's daughter, Moses might have been, if he had pleased, a very great man. If he had been content with the position in which he found himself at the Egyptian court, he might easily have been among the first —if not the very first—in all the land of Egypt.

Think, reader, for a moment, how great this temptation was.

Here was a man of like passions with ourselves. He might have had as much greatness as earth can well give. Rank, power, place, honour, titles, dignities—all were before him, and within his grasp. These are the things for which many men are continually struggling. These are the prizes which there is such an incessant race in the world around us to obtain. To be somebody —to be looked up to—to raise themselves in the scale of society—to get a handle to their names — these are the things for which many sacrifice time, and thought, and health, and life itself. But Moses would not have them at a gift. He turned his back upon them. He refused them. He gave them up.

2. And more than this, *he refused pleasure.*

Pleasure of every kind, no doubt, was at his feet, if he had liked to take it up—sensual pleasure—intellectual pleasure—social pleasure—whatever could strike his fancy. Egypt was a land of artists—a residence of learned men—a resort of everyone who had skill, or science of any description. There was nothing which could feed the lust of the flesh, the lust of the eye, or the pride of life, which one in the place of Moses might not easily have commanded.

Think again, reader, how great was this temptation also.

This, be it remembered, is the one thing for which millions live. They differ, perhaps, in their views of what makes up real pleasure—but all agree in seeking first and foremost to obtain it. Pleasure and enjoyment in the holidays is the grand object to which a school boy looks forward. Pleasure and satisfaction in making himself independent, is the mark on which the young man in business fixes his eye. Pleasure and ease in retiring from business with a fortune, is the aim which the merchant sets before him. Pleasure and bodily comfort at his own house is the sum of the poor man's wishes. Pleasure and fresh excitement in politics, in travelling, in amusements, in company, in books—this is the goal towards which the rich man is straining·

Pleasure is the shadow that all alike are hunting—high and low—rich and poor—old and young, one with another; each perhaps pretending to despise his neighbour for seeking it—each in his own way seeking it for himself—each secretly wondering that he does not find it—each firmly persuaded that somewhere or other it is to be found. This was the cup that Moses had before his lips. He might have drank as deeply as he liked of earthly pleasure. But he would not have it. He turned his back upon it. He refused it. He gave it up

3. And more than this, *he refused riches.*

"The Treasures in Egypt" is an expression that seems to tell of wealth that he might have enjoyed had he been content to remain with Pharaoh's daughter. We may well suppose these treasures would have been a mighty fortune. Enough is still remaining in Egypt to give us some faint idea of the money at its king's disposal. The pyramids, and obelisks, and statues, are still standing there as witnesses, The ruins at Carnac, and Luxor, and Denderah, and many other places, are still the mightiest buildings in the world. They testify to this day that the man who gave up Egyptian wealth, gave up something which even our English minds would find it hard to reckon up.

Think once more, how great was this temptation.

Consider, reader, the power of money—the immense influence that the love of money obtains over men's minds. Look around you and see how men covet it, and what amazing pains and trouble they will go through to obtain it. Tell them of an island many

thousand miles away, where something may be found
which may be profitable if imported, and at once a
fleet of ships will be sent to get it.   Show them a way
to make one per cent. more of their money, and they
will reckon you among the wisest of men—they will
almost fall down and worship you.   To possess money
seems to hide defects—to cover over faults—to clothe
a man with virtues.   People can get over much, if you
are rich.   But here is a man who might have been rich,
and would not.   He would not have Egyptian treasures.
He turned his back upon them.   He refused them
He gave them up.

Such were the things that Moses refused—rank,
pleasure, riches, all three at once.

Add to all this that he did it *deliberately*.   He did
not refuse these things in a hasty fit of youthful
excitement.   He was forty years old.   He was in the
prime of life.   He knew what he was about.   He
weighed both sides of the question.

Add to it that he did not refuse them *because he
was obliged*.   He was not like the dying man, who tells us
" He craves nothing more in this world ; " and why ?—
Because he is leaving the world, and cannot keep it.
He was not like the pauper, who makes a merit of
necessity, and says, " He does not want riches ; " and
why ?   Because he cannot get them.   He was not like
the old man, who boasts " that he has laid aside
worldly pleasures ; " and why ?   Because he is worn out,
and cannot enjoy them.   No ! reader.   Moses refused
what he might have kept, and gave up what he might

have enjoyed. Rank, pleasure, and riches did not leave him, but he left them.

And then judge whether I am not right in saying that his was one of the greatest sacrifices mortal man ever made. Others have refused much, but none, I think, so much as Moses. Others have done well in the way of self-sacrifice and self-denial, but he excels them all.

II. And now let me go on to the second thing I wish to set before you. I will speak of *what Moses chose.*

I think his choice as wonderful as his refusal. He chose three things for his soul's sake. The road to salvation led through them, and he followed it; and in so doing he chose three of the last things that man is ever disposed to take up.

1. For one thing *he chose suffering and affliction.*

He left the ease and comfort of Pharaoh's court, and openly took part with the children of Israel. They were an enslaved and persecuted people—an object of distrust, suspicion, and hatred; and the man who befriended them was sure to taste something of the bitter cup they were daily drinking.

To man's eye there seemed no chance of their deliverance from bondage without a long and doubtful struggle. A settled home and country for them must have appeared a thing never likely to be obtained, however much desired. In fact, if ever man seemed to be choosing pain, trials, poverty, want, distress, anxiety.

perhaps even death, with his eyes open, Moses was that man.

Think only, reader, how wonderful was this choice.

Man naturally shrinks from pain. It is in us all to do so. We draw back by a kind of instinct from suffering, and avoid it if we can. If two courses of action are set before us, which both seem right, we always take that which is the least disagreeable to flesh and blood. We spend our days in fear and anxiety, when we think affliction is coming near us, and use every means to escape it. And when it does come, we often fret and murmur under the burden of it ; and if we can but bear it patiently we count it a great matter indeed.

But look here. Here is a man of like passions with yourself, and he actually chooses affliction !

Moses saw the cup of suffering that was before him if he left Pharaoh's court, and he chose it, preferred it, and took it up.

2. But he did more than this, *he chose the company of a despised people.*

He left the society of the great and wise, among whom he had been brought up, and joined himself to the children of Israel. He who had lived from infancy in the midst of rank, and riches, and luxury, came down from his high estate, and cast in his lot with poor men —slaves, bondservants, oppressed, destitute, afflicted, tormented—labourers in the brick-kiln.

How wonderful, once more, was this choice !

Generally speaking we think it enough to carry our

own troubles. We may be sorry for others whose lot is to be mean and despised—we may even try to help them—we may give money to raise them—we may speak for them to those on whom they depend; but here we generally stop.

But here is a man who does far more. He not merely feels for despised Israel, but actually goes down to them, adds himself to their society, and lives with them altogether. You would wonder if some great man in Grosvenor or Belgrave Square were to give up house, and fortune, and position in society, and go to live on a small allowance in some narrow lane in Bethnal Green, for the sake of doing good : yet this would convey a very faint and feeble notion of the kind of thing that Moses did. He saw a despised people, and he chose their company in preference to that of the noblest in the land. He became one with them,—their fellow, their associate, and their friend.

3. But he did even more. *He chose reproach and scorn.*

Who can conceive the torrent of mockery and ridicule that Moses would have to stem, in turning away from Pharaoh's court to join Israel.

Men would tell him he was mad, foolish, weak, silly, out of his mind ; he would lose his influence ; he would forfeit the favour and good opinion of all among whom he had lived.

Think again, reader, what a choice this was ?

There are few things more powerful than ridicule and scorn. It can do far more than open enmity and persecution. Many a man who would march up to a cannon's mouth, or lead a forlorn hope, or storm a breach! has found it impossible to face the mockery of a few companions, and has flinched from the path of duty to avoid it. To be laughed at! To be made a joke of! To be jested and sneered at! To be reckoned weak and silly! To be thought a fool! There is nothing grand in all this, and they cannot make up their minds to undergo it.

Yet here is a man who made up his mind to it, and did not shrink from the trial. Moses saw reproach and scorn before him, and he chose them, and accepted them for his portion.

Such then were the things that Moses chose— affliction, the company of a despised people, and scorn.

Set down beside all this, that Moses was no weak, ignorant, illiterate person, who did not know what he was about. You are specially told he was a " learned " man, he was one " mighty in words and in deeds," and yet he chose as he did.

Set down, too, the circumstances of his choice. He was not obliged to choose as he did. None compelled him to take such a course. The things he took up did not force themselves upon him against his will. He went after them, they did not come after him. All that he did, he did of his own free choice, voluntarily and of his own accord.

And then judge whether it is not true that his choice was as wonderful as his refusal. Since the world began,

I suppose, none ever made such a choice as the man Moses did in our text.

III. And now let me go on to a third thing :—*let me speak of the principle which moved Moses, and made him do as he did.*

How can this conduct of his be accounted for ? What possible reason can be given for it ? To refuse that which is generally called a good—to choose that which is commonly thought an evil—this is not the way of flesh and blood—this is not the manner of man—this requires some explanation. What will that explanation be ?

You hear the answer in the text. I know not whether its greatness or its simplicity is more to be admired. It all lies in one little word, and that word is, " FAITH."

Moses had faith. Faith was the mainspring of his wonderful conduct. Faith made him do as he did, choose what he chose, and refuse what he refused. He did it all because he believed.

God set before the eyes of his mind His Own will and purpose. God revealed to him that a Saviour was to be born of the stock of Israel—that mighty promises were bound up in these children of Abraham, and yet to be fulfilled—that the time for fulfilling a portion of these promises was at hand—and Moses put credit in this, and believed. And every step in his wonderful career—every action in his journey through life, after leaving Pharaoh's court—his choice of seeming evil, his refusal of seeming good—all must be traced up to this

fountain, all will be found to rest on this foundation—
God had spoken to him, and he had faith in God's
word.

He believed that God would *keep his promises:* that
what He had said He would surely do; and what He had
covenanted He would surely perform.

He believed that with God *nothing was impossible.*
Reason and sense might say that the deliverance of
Israel was out of the question,—the obstacles were too
many, the difficulties too great. But faith told Moses
that God was all-sufficient. God had undertaken the
work, and it would be done.

He believed that God was *all wise.* Reason and sense
might tell him that his line of action was absurd; he
was throwing away useful influence, and destroying
the chance of benefitting his people, by breaking with
Pharaoh's daughter. But faith told Moses that if God
said, "Go this way," it must be the best.

He believed that God was *all merciful.* Reason and
sense might hint that a more pleasant manner of
deliverance might be found; that some compromise
might be effected, and many hardships be avoided. But
faith told Moses that God was love, and would not give
His people one drop of bitterness beyond what was
absolutely needed.

Faith was a *telescope* to Moses. It made him see
the goodly land afar off—rest, peace, victory—when
dim-sighted reason could only see trial and barrenness,
storm and tempest, weariness and pain.

Faith was an *interpreter* to Moses. It made him

pick out a comfortable meaning in the dark demands of God's handwriting, while ignorant sense could see nothing in it all but mystery and foolishness.

Faith told Moses that all this rank and greatness was of the earth, earthy; a poor, vain, empty thing, frail, fleeting, and passing away; and that there was no true greatness like that of serving God. He was the king, he the true nobleman who belonged to the family of God. It was better to be last in heaven, than first in hell.

Faith told Moses that worldly pleasures were pleasures of sin. They were mingled with sin—they led on to sin,—they were ruinous to the soul, and displeasing to God. It would be small comfort to have pleasure while God was against him. Better suffer and obey God, than be at ease and sin.

Faith told Moses that these pleasures after all were only for a season:—they could not last—they were all short-lived—they would weary him soon—he must leave them all in a few years.

Faith told him there was a reward in heaven for the believer far richer than the treasures in Egypt; durable riches, where rust could not corrupt, nor thieves break through and steal. The crown there would be incorruptible; the weight of glory would be exceeding and eternal; and faith bade him look away to that if his eyes were dazzled with Egyptian gold.

Faith told Moses that affliction and suffering were not real evils: they were the school of God, in which he trains the children of grace for glory; the medicines which are needful to purify our corrupt wills; the furnace which must burn away our dross; the knife which must cut loose the ties that bind us to the world.

Faith told Moses that this despised people were the people of God; that to them belonged the adoption, and covenant, and the promises, and the glory; that of them the seed of the woman was one day to be born, who should bruise the serpent's head; that the special blessing of God was upon them; that they were lovely and beautiful in his eyes; and that it was better to be a door-keeper among the people of God, than to reign in the palaces of wickedness.

Faith told Moses that all the reproach and scorn poured out on him was the reproach of Christ; that it was honourable to be mocked and despised for Christ's sake; that whoso persecuted Christ's people was persecuting Christ Himself; and that the day must come when His enemies would bow before Him and lick the dust.

All this, and much more, of which I cannot speak particularly, Moses saw by faith. These were the things he believed, and believing did what he did: He was persuaded of them, and embraced them, he reckoned them as certainties, he regarded them as substantial verities, he counted them as sure as if he had seen them with his eyes, he acted on them as realities, and this made him the man that he was.

Marvel not that he refused greatness, riches, and pleasure. He looked far forward. He saw with the eye of faith kingdoms crumbling into dust, riches making to themselves wings and fleeing away, pleasures leading on to death and judgment, and Christ only and His little flock enduring for ever.

Wonder not that he chose affliction, a despised people, and reproach. He beheld things below the surface. He saw with the eye of faith affliction lasting but for a moment, reproach rolled away, and ending in everlasting honour, and the despised people of God reigning as kings with Christ in glory.

And, reader, was he not right ?   Does he not speak to us, though dead, this very day ?   The name of Pharaoh's daughter has perished ; the city where Pharaoh reigned is not known ; the treasures in Egypt are gone : but the name of Moses is known wherever the Bible is read, and is still a standing witness that whoso liveth by faith, happy is he.

IV.   And now let me wind up all by trying to set before you some *practical lessons, which appear to me to follow from this text.*

What has all this to do with us ? some men will say. We do not live in Egypt, we have seen no miracles; we are not Israelites, we are weary of the subject.

Stay a little, reader, if this be the thought of your heart, and by God's help I will show you that all may learn here, and all may be instructed.

1.   For one thing, *if ever you would be saved, you must make the choice that Moses made,—you must prefer God before the world.*

Reader, mark well what I say. Do not overlook this, though all the rest be forgotten. I do not say that the statesman must throw up his office, and the rich man forsake his property. Let no one fancy that I mean this. But I say, if a man would be saved, whatever be his rank in life, he must be prepared for tribulation; they must make up his mind to choose that which is evil, and to give up and refuse that which seems good.

I dare be sure this sounds strange language to some who read these pages. I know well you may have a certain form of religion, and find no trouble in your way. There is a common worldly kind of Christianity in this day, which many have, and think they have enough—a cheap Christianity which offends nobody, and requires no sacrifice, which costs nothing, and is worth nothing. I am not speaking of religion of this kind.

But if you really are in earnest about your soul, if your religion is something more than a mere fashionable cloak, if you are determined to live by the Bible, if you are resolved to be a New Testament Christian, then, I repeat, you will soon find you must carry a cross, you must endure hard things, you must suffer because of your soul, as Moses did, or you cannot be saved.

The world in the nineteenth century is what it always was. The hearts of men are still the same. The offence of the cross is not ceased. God's true people are still a despised little flock. True evangelical religion still brings with it reproach and scorn. A real servant of God will still be thought by many a weak enthusiast and a fool.

Reader, do you wish your soul to be saved? Then remember, you must choose whom you will serve. You cannot serve God and mammon. You cannot be on two sides at once. You cannot be a friend of Christ, and a friend of the world at the same time. You must come out from the children of this world, and be separate; you must put up with much ridicule, trouble, and opposition, or you are lost for ever. You must be willing to think and do things which the world considers foolish, and to hold opinions which are only held by a few. It will cost you something. The stream is strong, and you have to stem it. The way is narrow and steep, and it is no use saying it is not. But depend on it, there can be no saving religion without sacrifices and self-denial.

Now, reader, are you doing anything of this kind? I put it to your conscience in all affection and tenderness, are you, like Moses, preferring God to the world, or not? I beseech you not to take shelter under that dangerous word "we," — "we ought," and "we hope," and "we mean," and the like. I ask you plainly, what are you doing yourself? Are you willing to give up anything which keeps you back from God? or are you clinging to the Egypt of the world, and saying to yourself, "I must have it; I must have it; I cannot tear myself away?" What sacrifices are you making? Are you making any at all? Is there any cross in your Christianity? Are there any sharp corners in your

N

religion, anything that ever jars and comes in collision
with the earthly-mindedness around you, or is all smooth
and rounded off, and comfortably fitted into custom and
fashion? Do you know anything of the afflictions of
the Gospel? Is your faith and practice ever a subject
of scorn and reproach? Are you thought a fool by any
one because of your soul? Have you left Pharaoh's
daughter, and heartily joined the people of God? Are
you venturing all on Christ? Search and see.

Reader, these are hard and rough sayings. I cannot
help it. I believe they are founded on Scripture truths.
I remember it is written, "There went great multitudes
with Jesus; and he turned, and said unto them, If any
man come to me, and hate not his father, and mother,
and wife, and children, and brethren, and sisters, yea,
and his own life also, he cannot be my disciple. And
whosoever doth not bear his cross, and come after me,
cannot be my disciple." (Luke xiv. 25, 27.) Many, I
fear, would like glory, who have no wish for grace—
they would fain have the wages, but not the work, the
harvest, but not the labour, the reaping, but not the
sowing, the reward, but not the battle. But it may
not be. As Bunyan says, "the bitter must go before
the sweet." If there is no cross there will be no crown.

2. The second thing I will say is this—*nothing
will ever enable you to choose God before the world
except faith.*

Nothing else will do it. Knowledge will not ;
feeling will not; a regular use of outward forms will
not; good companions will not. All these may do

something, but the fruit they produce has no power of continuance, it will not last. A religion springing from such sources will only endure so long as there is no tribulation or persecution because of the word; but so soon as there is any, it will dry up. It is a clock without weights—its face may be beautiful, you may turn its fingers round, but it will not go.

A religion that is to stand must have a living foundation, and there is none other but faith.

Reader, have you got this faith? If you have, you will find it possible to refuse seeming good, and choose seeming evil—you will think nothing of to-day's losses, in the hope of to-morrow's gains—you will follow Christ in the dark, and stand by Him to the very last. If you have not, I warn you, you will never war a good warfare, and so run as to obtain—you will soon be offended and turn back to the world.

There must be a real belief that God's promises are sure and to be depended on; a real belief that what God says in the Bible is all true, and that every doctrine contrary to this is false, whoever may say it. There must be a real belief that all God's words are to be received, however hard and disa reeable to flesh and blood, and that His way is right, and all others wrong; this there must be, or you will never come out from the world, take up the cross, follow Christ and be saved.

You must learn to believe promises better than possession; things unseen better than things s en things in heaven out of sight, better than things on earth before your eyes; the praise of the invisib le God

better than the praise of visible man. Then, and then
only, you will make a choice like Moses, and prefer God
to the world.

This was the faith by which the old saints obtained a
good report.   This was the weapon by which they
overcame the world.   This made them what they were.

This was the faith that made Noah go on building
his ark, while the world looked on and mocked—
and Abraham give the choice of the land to Lot, and
dwell on quietly in tents—and Ruth cleave to Naomi,
and turn away from her country and her gods—and
Daniel continue in prayer, though he knew the lions'
den was prepared—and the three children refuse to
worship idols, though the fiery furnace was before
their eyes.   All these acted as they did because they
believed.   Well may the Apostle Peter speak of faith
as "precious faith"   (2 Peter i. 1).

3.   The third thing I shall say is this, *the true
reason why so many are worldly and ungodly
persons is, that they have no faith.*

Reader, you must be aware that multitudes of professing Christians would never think for a moment of
doing as Moses did.   It is useless to speak smooth
things, and shut our eyes to the fact.   That man must
be blind who does not see thousands around him who
are daily preferring the world to God—placing the
things of time before the things of eternity—the things
of the body before the things of the soul.   You may not
like to hear it, but so it is.

And why do they do so?   No doubt they will all

give us reasons and excuses. Some will talk of the snares of the world, some of the want of time, some of the peculiar difficulties of their position, some of the cares and anxieties of life, some of the strength of temptation, some of the power of passions, some of the effects of bad companions. But what does it come to after all? There is a far shorter way to account for the state of their souls, *they do not believe.* One simple sentence, like Aaron's rod, will swallow up all their excuses, *they have no faith.*

They do not really think what God says is true. They secretly flatter themselves with the notion, " It will surely not be fulfilled, all of it; there must surely be some other way to heaven besides that which ministers speak of; there cannot surely be so much danger of being lost." In short they do not put implicit confidence in the words that God has written and spoken, and so do not act upon them. They do not thoroughly believe in hell, and so do not flee from it; nor heaven, and so do not seek it; nor the guilt of sin, and so do not turn from it; nor the holiness of God, and so do not fear Him; nor their need of Christ, and so do not trust in Him, nor love Him. They do not feel confidence in God, and so venture nothing for Him. Like the boy Passion, in Pilgrim's Progress, they must have their good things now. They do not trust God, and so they cannot wait.

Reader, how is it with yourself? Do you believe all the Bible? Ask yourself that question. Depend on it, it is a much greater thing to believe all the Bible than

many suppose.   Happy is the man who can say, " I am
a believer."

We talk of infidels sometimes as if they were the
rarest people in the world.   And I grant you that open
avowed infidelity is happily not common now.   But
there is a vast amount of practical infidelity around us,
for all that, which is as dangerous in the end as the
principles of Voltaire and Paine.   There are many who
Sunday after Sunday repeat their creed, and make a
point of declaring their belief in all that the Apostolic
and Nicene forms contain, and yet these very persons
will live all the week as if Christ had never died, and as
if there were no judgment, and no resurrection of the
dead, and no life everlasting at all.   There are many
who will say, " Oh, we know it all," when spoken to
about eternal things, and the value of their souls ; and
yet their lives show plainly they know not anything as
they ought to know ; and the saddest part of their state
is, that they think they do.

Reader, I warn you that knowledge not acted upon,
in God's sight, is no knowledge at all.   A faith that
does not influence a man's practice is not worthy of the
name.   There are only two classes in the church of
Christ—those who believe, and those who do not. The
difference between the true Christian and the mere
outward professor just lies in one word ; the true
Christian is like Moses, " he has faith ; " the professor
has none.   The true Christian believes, and therefore
lives as he does ; the mere professor does not believe,

and therefore is what he is. Oh! where is your faith?
Be not faithless, but believing.

4. The last thing I will say is this, *the true secret
of doing great things for God is, to have great faith.*

I suspect that we are all apt to err a little on this
point. We think too much, and talk too much about
graces, and gifts, and attainments, and do not
sufficiently remember that faith is the root and mother
of them all. In walking with God, a man will go just
as far as he believes, and no further. His life will
always be proportioned to his faith. His peace, his
patience, his courage, his zeal, his works—all will be
according to his faith.

You read the lives of eminent Christians perhaps.
Such men as Romaine, or Newton, or Martyn, Scott,
or Simeon, or M'Cheyne; and you are disposed to say,
"What wonderful gifts and graces these men had!"
I answer, you should rather give honour to the mother-
grace which God puts forward in the eleventh chapter
of the Epistle to the Hebrews — you should give
honour to their faith. Depend on it, faith was the
mainspring in the character of each and all.

I can fancy some one saying, "They were so prayerful; that made them what they were." I answer,
why did they pray much? Simply because they
had much faith. What is prayer, but faith speaking to
God?

Another perhaps will say, "They were so diligent
and laborious—that accounts for their success." I
answer, why were they so diligent? Simply because

they had faith.   What is Christian diligence, but faith at work ?

Another will tell me, "They were so bold— that rendered them so useful." I answer, why were they so bold ? Simply because they had much faith. What is Christian boldness, but faith honestly doing its duty ?

And another will cry, " It was their holiness and spirituality—that gave them their weight." For the last time I answer, what made them holy ? Nothing but a living realizing spirit of faith. What is holiness, but faith visible and faith incarnate ?

Now, dear reader, would you grow in grace, and in the knowledge of our Lord Jesus Christ ? Would you bring forth much fruit ? Would you be eminently useful ? Would you be bright, and shine as a light in your day ? Would you, like Moses, make it clear as noonday that you have chosen God before the world ! I dare be sure that every believer will reply : " Yes yes ! yes ! these are the things we long for and desire."

Then take the advice I give you this day :—go and cry to the Lord Jesus Christ, as the disciples did, " Lord, increase our faith." Faith is the root of a real Christian's character. Let your root be right, and your fruit will soon abound. Your spiritual prosperity will always be according to your faith. He that believeth shall not only be saved, but shall never thirst—shall overcome—shall be established—shall walk firmly on the waters of this world—and shall do great works.

"COME OUT, AND BE YE SEPARATE."

" COME OUT, AND BE YE SEPARATE."

"Come out from among them, and be ye separate, saith the Lord" (2 COR. vi. 17).

THE words which head this page touch a subject of vast importance in religion. That subject is the great duty of separation from the world. This is the point which St. Paul had in view when he wrote to the Corinthians, " Come out —be separate."

The subject is one which demands the best attention of all who profess and call themselves Christians. In every age of the Church separation from the world has always been one of the grand evidences of a work of grace in the heart. He that has been really born of the Spirit, and made a new creature in Christ Jesus, has always endeavoured to " come out from the world," and live a separate life. They who have only had the name of Christian without the reality, have always refused to " come out and be separate " from the world.

The subject perhaps was never more important than it is at the present day. There is a widely-spread desire to make things pleasant in religion—to saw off the corners and edges of the cross, and to avoid, as far as possible, self-denial. On every side we hear professing Christians declaring loudly that we must not be " narrow and exclusive," and that there is no harm in many things which the holiest saints of old thought bad for their souls. That we may go anywhere, and do anything, and spend our time in anything, and read anything, and keep any company, and plunge into anything, and all the while may be very good Christians—this, this is the maxim of thousands. In a day like this I think it good to raise a warning voice, and invite attention to the teaching of God's Word. It is written in that Word, "Come out, and be separate."

There are four points which I shall try to show my readers in examining this mighty subject.

I. First, I shall try to show *that the world is a source of great danger to the soul.*

II. Secondly, I shall try to show *what is not meant by separation from the world.*

III. Thirdly, I shall try to show in *what real separation from the world consists.*

IV. Fourthly, I shall try *to show the secret of victory over the world.*

And now, before I go a single step further, let me warn every reader of this paper that he will never understand this subject unless he first understands what a true Christian is. If you are one of those unhappy people who think everybody is a Christian who goes to a place of worship, no matter how he lives, or what he believes, I fear you will care little about separation from the world. But if you read your Bible, and are in earnest about your soul, you will know that there are two classes of Christians—converted and un-

converted. You will know that what the Jews were
among the nations under the Old Testament, this the
true Christian is meant to be under the New. You
will understand what I mean when I say that true
Christians are meant, in like manner, to be a "peculiar
people" under the Gospel, and that there must be a
difference between believers and unbelievers. To you,
therefore, I make a special appeal this day. While
many avoid the subject of separation from the world,
and many positively hate it, and many are puzzled by
it, give me your attention while I try to show you the
thing as it is.

I. First of all, let me show that *the world is a
source of great danger to the soul.*

By the world, be it remembered, I do not mean
the material world on the face of which we are living
and moving. He that pretends to say that anything
which God has created in the heavens above, or the
earth beneath, is in itself harmful to man's soul, says
that which is unreasonable and absurd. On the
contrary, the sun, moon, and stars,—the mountains,
the valleys, and the plains,—the seas, lakes, and rivers,
—the animal and vegetable creation,—all are in themselves very good. All are full of lessons of God's
wisdom and power, and all proclaim daily, "The hand
that made us is divine." The idea that "matter" is
in itself sinful and corrupt is a foolish heresy.

When I speak of "the world" in this paper, I mean
those people who think only, or chiefly, of this world's

things, and neglect the world to come,—the people who are always thinking more of earth than of heaven, more of time than of eternity, more of the body than of the soul, more of pleasing man than of pleasing God. It is of them and their ways, habits, customs, opinions, practices, tastes, aims, spirit, and tone, that I am speaking when I speak of "the world." This is the world from which St. Paul tells us to "Come out and be separate."

Now that the world, in this sense, is an enemy to the soul, the well-known Church Catechism teaches us at its very beginning. It tells us that there are three things which a baptized Christian is bound to renounce and give up, and three enemies which he ought to fight with and resist. These three are the flesh, the devil, and the world. All three are terrible foes, and all three must be overcome, if we would be saved.

But, whatever men please to think about the Catechism, we shall do well to turn to the testimony of Holy Scripture. If the texts I am about to quote do not prove that the world is a source of danger to the soul, there is no meaning in words.

(a) Let us hear what St. Paul says :—

" Be not conformed to this world : but be ye transformed by the renewing of your mind " (Rom. xii. 2).

"We have received, not the spirit of the world, but the spirit which is of God " (1 Cor. ii. 12).

Christ "gave Himself for our sins, that He might deliver us from this present evil world " (Gal. i. 4).

"In time past ye walked according to the course of this world" (Eph. ii. 2).

"Demas hath forsaken me, having loved this present world" (2 Tim. iv. 10).

(b) Let us hear what St. James says :—

"Pure religion and undefiled before God and the Father, is this, To visit the fatherless and widows in their affliction, and to keep himself unspotted from the world" (James i. 27).

"Know ye not that the friendship of the world is enmity with God ? Whosover therefore will be a friend of the world, is the enemy of God" (James iv. 4).

(c) Let us hear what St. John says :—

"Love not the world, neither the things that are in the world. If any man love the world, the love of the Father is not in him.

"For all that is in the world, the lust of the flesh, and the lust of the eyes, and the pride of life, is not of the Father, but is of the world.

"And the world passeth away, and the lust thereof; but he that doeth the will of God abideth for ever" (1 John ii. 15-17),

"The world knoweth us not, because it knew Him not" (1 John iii. 1).

"They are of the world : therefore speak they of the world, and the world heareth them " (1 John iv. 5).

"Whatsoever is born of God overcometh the world" (1 John v. 4).

" We know that we are of God, and the whole world lieth in wickedness " (1 John v. 19).

(d) Let us hear lastly what the Lord Jesus Christ says :—

" The care of this world . . . choke the word, and he becometh unfruitful " (Matt. xiii. 22).

" Ye are of this world : I am not of this world " (John viii. 23).

" The Spirit of truth ; whom the world cannot receive, because it seeth Him not, neither knoweth Him " (John xiv. 17).

" If the world hate you, ye know that it hated Me before it hated you " (John xv. 18).

" If ye were of the world, the world would love his own : but because ye are not of the world, but I have chosen you out of the world, therefore the world hateth you " (John xv. 19).

" In the world ye shall have tribulation : but be of good cheer ; I have overcome the world " (John xvi. 33).

" They are not of the world, even as I am not of the world " (John xvii. 16).

I make no comment on these twenty-two texts. They speak for themselves. If any one can read them carefully, and fail to see that the world is an enemy to the Christian, and that there is an utter opposition between the friendship of the world and the friendship of Christ, he is past the reach of argument, and it is waste of time to reason with him.

To my eyes they contain a lesson as clear as the sun at noonday.

I turn from Scripture to matters of fact and experience. I appeal to any old Christian who keeps his eyes open, and knows what is going on in the churches. I ask him whether it be not true that nothing damages the cause of religion so much as "the world!" It is not open sin, or open unbelief, which robs Christ of His professing servants, so much as the love of the world, the fear of the world, the cares of the world, the business of the world, the money of the world, the pleasures of the world, and the desire to keep in with the world. This is the great rock on which thousands of young people are continually making shipwreck. They do not object to any article of the Christian faith. They do not deliberately choose evil, and openly rebel against God. They hope somehow to get to heaven at last; and they think it proper to have some religion. But they cannot give up their idol: they must have the world. And so, after running well and bidding fair for heaven while boys and girls, they turn aside when they become men and women, and go down the broad way which leads to destruction. They begin with Abraham and Moses, and end with Demas and Lot's wife.

The last day alone will prove how many souls the world has slain. Hundreds will be found to have been trained in religious families, and to have known the Gospel from their very childhood, and yet missed heaven. They left the harbour of home with bright

o

prospects, and launched forth on the ocean of life with a father's blessing and a mother's prayers, and then got out of the right course through the seductions of the world, and ended their voyage in shallows and in misery. It is a sorrowful story to tell; but, alas, it is only too common! I cannot wonder that St. Paul says, "Come out and be separate."

II. Let me now try to show *what does not constitute separation from the world.*

The point is one which requires clearing up. There are many mistakes made about it. You will sometimes see sincere and well-meaning Christians doing things which God never intended them to do, in the matter of separation from the world, and honestly believing that they are in the path of duty. Their mistakes often do great harm. They give occasion to the wicked to ridicule all religion and supply them with an excuse for having none. They cause the way of truth to be evil spoken of, and add to the offence of the cross. I think it a plain duty to make a few remarks on the subject. We must never forget that it is possible to be very much in earnest, and to think we are "doing God service," when in reality we are making some great mistake. There is such a thing as "zeal not according to knowledge." There are few things on which it is so important to pray for a right judgment and Christian common sense, as about separation from the world.

(*a*) When St. Paul said, "Come out and be separate," he did not mean that Christians ought to give up all

callings, trades, professions, and worldly business.
He did not forbid men to be soldiers, sailors, lawyers,
doctors, merchants, bankers, shopkeepers, or trades-
men. There is not a word in the New Testament
to justify such a line of conduct. Cornelius the
centurion, Luke the physician, Zenas the lawyer, are
examples to the contrary. Idleness is in itself a sin.
A lawful calling is a remedy against temptation. "If
any man will not work, neither shall he eat" (2
Thess. iii. 10). To give up any business of life, which
is not necessarily sinful, to the wicked and the devil,
from fear of getting harm from it, is lazy cowardly
conduct. The right plan is to carry our religion into
our business, and not to give up business under the
specious pretence that it interferes with our religion.

(b) When St. Paul said, "Come out and be separate,"
he did not mean that Christians ought to decline all
intercourse with unconverted people, and refuse to go
into their society. There is no warrant for such
conduct in the New Testament. Our Lord and His
disciples did not refuse to go to a marriage feast, or
to sit at meat at a Pharisee's table. St. Paul does not
say, "If any of them that believe not bid you to a
feast," you must not go, but only tells us how to
behave if we do go (1 Cor. x. 27). Moreover, it
is a dangerous thing to begin judging people too
closely, and settling who are converted and who are
not, and what society is godly and what ungodly.
We are sure to make mistakes. Above all, such a
course of life would cut us off from many opportunities

of doing good. If we carry our Master with us
wherever we go, who can tell but we may save some,
and get no harm ?

(c) When St. Paul says "Come out and be separate"
he does not mean that Christians ought to take no
interest in anything on earth except religion. To
neglect science, art, literature, and politics,—to read
nothing which is not directly spiritual,—to know
nothing about what is going on among mankind, and
never to look at a newspaper,—to care nothing about
the government of one's country, and to be utterly
indifferent as to the persons who guide its counsels
and make its laws,—all this may seem very right
and proper in the eyes of some people. But I take
leave to think that it is an idle, selfish neglect of duty.
St. Paul knew the value of good government, as
one of the main helps to our " living a quiet and
peaceable life in all godliness and honesty " (1 Tim. ii. 2).
St. Paul was not ashamed to read heathen writers,
and to quote their words in his speeches and writing.
St. Paul did not think it beneath him to show an
acquaintance with the laws and customs and callings
of the world, in the illustrations he gave from them.
Christians who plume themselves on their ignorance
of secular things are precisely the Christians who
bring religion into contempt. I knew the case of a
blacksmith who would not come to hear his clergyman
preach the Gospel, until he found out that he knew
the properties of iron. Then he came.

(d) When St. Paul said, " Come out and be separate,"

he did not mean that Christians should be singular, eccentric, and peculiar in their dress, manners, demeanour and voice. Anything which attracts notice in these matters is most objectionable, and ought to be carefully avoided. To wear clothes of such a colour, or made in such a fashion, that when you go into company every eye is fixed on you, and you are the object of general observation, is an enormous mistake. It gives occasion to the wicked to ridicule religion, and looks self-righteous and affected. There is not the slightest proof that our Lord and His apostles, and Priscilla, and Persis, and their companions, did not dress and behave just like others in their own ranks of life. On the other hand, one of the many charges our Lord brings against the Pharisees was that of making broad their phylacteries, and enlarging the borders of their garments, so as to be " seen of men " (Matt. xxiii. 5). True sanctity and sanctimoniousness are entirely different things. Those who try to show their unworldliness by wearing conspicuously ugly clothes, or by speaking in a whining, snuffling voice, or by affecting an unnatural slavishness, humility, and gravity of manner, miss their mark altogether, and only give occasion to the enemies of the Lord to blaspheme.

(e) When St. Paul said " Come out and be separate, " he did not mean that Christians ought to retire from the company of mankind, and shut themselves up in solitude. It is one of the crying errors of the Church of Rome to suppose that eminent holiness is to be attained by such practices. It is the unhappy delusion of the whole army of monks, nuns, and hermits. Separation of this kind is not according to the mind of Christ. He says distinctly in His last prayer, "I pray not that Thou shouldest take them out of the world, but that Thou shouldest keep them from the evil" (John xvii. 15). There is not a word in the Acts or Epistles to recommend such a separation. True believers are always represented as mixing in the world, doing their duty in it, and glorifying God by patience, meekness, purity, and courage in their several positions, and not by cowardly desertion of them. Moreover, it is foolish to suppose that we can keep the world and the devil out of our hearts by going into holes and corners True religion and unworldliness are best seen, not in timidly forsaking the post which God has allotted to us, but in manfully standing our ground, and showing the power of grace to overcome evil.

(f) Last, but not least, when St. Paul said, "Come out and be separate," he did not mean that Christians ought to withdraw from every Church in which there are unconverted members, or to refuse to worship in company with any who are not believers, or to keep away from the Lord's table if any ungodly people go up to it. This is a very common but a very grievous mistake. There is not a text in the New Testament to justify it, and it ought to be condemned as a pure invention of man. Our Lord Jesus Christ Himself deliberately allowed Judas Iscariot to be an apostle for three years, and gave him the Lord's Supper. He has taught us in the parable of the wheat and tares that converted and unconverted will be together till the harvest, and cannot be divided. In his Epistles to the Seven Churches, and in all St. Paul's Epistles, we often see faults and corruptions mentioned and reproved, but we are never told that they justify desertion of the assembly, or neglect of ordinances. In short, we must not look for a perfect Church, a perfect congregation, and a perfect company of communicants until the marriage supper of the Lamb. If others are unworthy Churchmen, or unworthy partakers of the Lord's Supper, the sin is theirs and not ours : we are not their judges. But to separate ourselves from Church assemblies, and deprive ourselves of Christian ordin-ances, because others use them unworthily, is to take up a foolish, unreasonable, and unscriptural position. It is not the mind of Christ, and it certainly is not St. Paul's idea of separation from the world.

I commend these six points to the calm considera-tion of all who wish to understand the subject of separation from the world. About each and all of them far more might be said than I have space to say in this paper. About each and all of them I have seen so many mistakes made, and so much misery and unhappiness caused by those mistakes, that I want to put Christians on their guard. I want them not to take up positions hastily, in the zeal of their first love, which they will afterwards be obliged to give up.

I leave this part of my subject with two pieces of advice, which I offer especially to young Christians.

I advise them, for one thing, if they really desire to come out from the world, to remember that the shortest path is not always the path of duty. To quarrel with all our unconverted relatives, to cut all our old friends, to withdraw entirely from mixed society, to live an exclusive life, to give up every act of courtesy and civility for the direct work of Christ—all this may seem very right, and may satisfy our consciences and save us trouble. But I venture a doubt whether it is not often a selfish, lazy, self-pleasing line of conduct, and whether the true cross and the true line of duty may not be to deny ourselves, and adopt a very different course of action. I advise them, for another thing, if they want to come out from the world, to watch against a sour, morose, ungenial, gloomy, unpleasant, bearish demeanour, and never to forget that there is such a thing as " winning without the Word" (1 Peter iii. 1). Let them strive to show unconverted people that their principles, whatever may be thought of them, make them cheerful, amiable, good-tempered, unselfish, considerate for others, and ready to take an interest in everything that is innocent and of good report. In short, let there be no needless separation between us and the world. In many things, as I shall soon show, we must be separate; but let us take care that it is separation of the right sort. If the world is offended by such separation we cannot help it. But let us never give the world occasion to say that our separation is foolish, senseless, ridiculous, unreasonable, uncharitable, and unscriptural.

III. In the third place I shall try to show *what true separation from the world really is.*

I take up this branch of my subject with a very deep sense of its difficulty, That there is a certain line of conduct which all true Christians ought to pursue with respect to " the world, and the things of the world," is very evident. The texts already quoted make that plain. The key to the solution of that question lies in the word "separation." But in what separation consists it is not easy to show. On some points it is not hard to lay down particular rules; on others it is impossible to do more than state general principles, and leave every one to apply them according to his position in life. This is what I shall now attempt to do.

(a) First and foremost, he that desires to " come out from the world, and be separate," *must steadily and habitually refuse to be guided by the world's standard of right and wrong.*

The rule of the bulk of mankind is to go with the stream, to do as others, to follow the fashion, to keep in with the common opinion, and to set your watch by the town clock. The true Christian will never be content with such a rule as that. He will simply ask, What saith the Scripture ? What is written in the Word of God ? He will maintain firmly that nothing can be right which God says is wrong, and that the custom and opinion of his neighbours can never make that to be a trifle which God calls serious, or that to be no sin which God calls sin. He will never think lightly of such sins as drinking, swearing, gambling, lying, cheating, swindling, or breach of the seventh commandment, because they are common, and many say, Where is the mighty harm? That miserable argument—"Everybody thinks so, everybody says so, everybody does it, everybody will be there," goes for nothing with him. Is it condemned or approved by the Bible? That is his only question. If he stands alone in the parish, or town, or congregation, he will not go against the Bible. If he has to come out from the crowd, and take a position by himself, he will not flinch from it rather than disobey the Bible. This is genuine Scriptural separation.

(b) He that desires to "come out from the world, and be separate," *must be very careful how he spends his leisure time.*

This is a point which at first sight appears of little importance. But the longer I live the more I am persuaded that it deserves most serious attention. Honourable occupation and lawful business are a great safeguard to the soul, and the time that is spent upon them is comparatively the time of our least danger. The devil finds it hard to get a hearing from a busy man. But when the day's work is over, and the time of leisure arrives, then comes the hour of temptation.

I do not hesitate to warn every man who wants to live a Christian life, to be very careful how he spends his evenings. Evening is the time when we are naturally disposed to unbend after the labours of the day; and evening is the time when the Christian is too often tempted to lay aside his armour, and consequently gets trouble on his soul. "Then cometh the devil," and with the devil the world. Evening is the time when the poor man is tempted to go to the public-house, and fall into sin. Evening is the time when the tradesman too often goes to the inn parlour, and sits for hours hearing and seeing things which do him no good. Evening is the time which the higher classes choose for dancing, card playing, and the like; and consequently never get to bed till late at night. If we love our souls, and would not become worldly, let us mind how we spend our evenings. Tell me how a man spends his evenings, and I can generally tell what his character is.

The true Christian will do well to make it a settled rule never to waste his evenings. Whatever others may do, let him resolve always to make time for quiet, calm thought—for Bible-reading and prayer. The rule will prove a hard one to keep. It may bring on him the charge of being unsocial and over-strict. Let him not mind this. Anything of this kind is better than habitual late hours in company, hurried prayers, slovenly Bible-reading, and a bad conscience. Even if he stands alone in his parish or town, let him not depart from his rule. He will find himself in a minority, and be thought a peculiar man. But this is genuine Scriptural separation.

(c) He that desires to "come out from the world, and be separate," must *steadily and habitually deter-*

mine not to be swallowed up and absorbed in the business of the world.

A true Christian will strive to do his duty in whatever station or position he finds himself, and to do it well. Whether statesman, or merchant, or banker, or lawyer, or doctor, or tradesman, or farmer, he will try to do his work so that no one can find occasion for fault in him. But he will not allow it to get between him and Christ. If he finds his business beginning to eat up his Sundays, his Bible-reading, his private prayer, and to bring clouds between him and heaven, he will say, "Stand back ! There is a limit. Hitherto thou mayest go, but no further. I cannot sell my soul for place, fame, or gold." Like Daniel, he will make time for his communion with God, whatever the cost may be. Like Havelock, he will deny himself anything rather than lose his Bible-reading and his prayers. In all this he will find he stands almost alone. Many will laugh at him, and tell him they get on well enough without being so strict and particular. He will heed it not. He will resolutely hold the world at arm's length, whatever present loss or sacrifice it may seen to entail. He will choose rather to be less rich and prosperous in this world, than not to prosper about his soul. To stand alone in this way, to run counter to the ways of others, requires immense self-denial. But this is genuine Scriptural separation.

(d) He that desires to "come out from the world, and be separate" must steadily *abstain from all*

amusements and recreations which are inseparably connected with sin.

This is a hard subject to handle, and I approach it with pain. But I do not think I should be faithful to Christ, and faithful to my office as a minister, if I did not speak very plainly about it, in considering such a matter as separation from the world.

Let me, then, say honestly, that I cannot understand how any one who makes any pretence to real vital religion, can allow himself to attend races and theatres. Conscience, no doubt, is a strange thing, and every man must judge for himself and use his liberty. One man sees no harm in things which another regards with abhorrence as evil. I can only give my own opinion for what it is worth, and entreat my readers to consider seriously what I say.

That to look at horses running at full speed is in itself perfectly harmless, no sensible man will pretend to deny. That many plays, such as Shakespeare's, are among the finest productions of the human intellect, is equally undeniable. But all this is beside the question. The question is whether horse-racing and theatres in England are not inseparably bound up with things that are downright wicked. I assert without hesitation that they are so bound up. I assert that the breach of God's commandments so invariably accompanies the race and the play, that you cannot go to the amusement without helping sin.

I entreat all professing Christians to remember this, and to take heed what they do. I warn them plainly that they have no right to shut their eyes to facts which every intelligent person knows, for the mere pleasure of seeing a horse-race, or listening to good actors or actresses. I warn them that they must not talk of separation from the world, if they can lend their sanction to amusements which are invariably connected with gambling, betting, drunkenness, and fornication. These are the things which God will judge. The end of these things is death.

Hard words these, no doubt! But are they not true? It may seem to your relatives and friends very strait-laced, strict, and narrow, if you tell them you cannot go to the races or the theatre with them. But we must fall back on first principles. Is the world a danger to the soul or is it not? Are we to come out from the world or are we not? These are questions which can only be answered in one way.

If we love our souls we must have nothing to do with amusements which are bound up with sin. Nothing short of this can be called genuine Scriptural separation from the world.

(e) He that desires to "come out from the world, and be separate," must be *moderate in the use of lawful and innocent recreations.*

No sensible Christian will ever think of condemning all recreations. In a world of wear and tear like that we live in, occasional unbending and relaxation are good for all. Body and mind alike require seasons of lighter occupation, and opportunities of letting off high spirits, and especially when they are young. Exercise itself is a positive necessity for the preservation of mental and bodily health. I see no harm in cricket, rowing, running, and other manly athletic recreations. I find no fault with those who play at chess and such-like games of skill. We are all fearfully and wonder-fully made. No wonder the poet says—

> "Strange that a harp of thousand strings
> Should keep in tune so long."

Anything which strengthens nerves, and brain, and digestion, and lungs, and muscles, and makes us more fit for Christ's work, so long as it is not in itself sinful, is a blessing, and ought to be thankfully used. Any-thing which will occasionally divert our thoughts from their usual grinding channel in a healthy manner, is a good and not an evil.

But it is the excess of these innocent things which a true Christian must watch against, if he wants to be separate from the world. He must not devote his whole heart, and soul, and mind, and strength, and time to them, as many do, if he wishes to serve Christ. There are hundreds of lawful things which are good in moderation, but bad when taken in excess: healthful medicine in small quantities—downright poison when swallowed down in huge doses. In nothing is this so true as it is in the matter of recrea-tions. The use of them is one thing, and the abuse of them is another. The Christian who uses them must know when to stop, and how to say Hold! enough! Do they interfere with his private religion? Do they

take up too much of his thoughts and attention ? Have
they a secularizing effect on his soul ? Have they a
tendency to pull him down to earth ? Then let him hold
hard and take care. All this will require courage, self-
denial, and firmness. It is a line of conduct which will
often bring on us the ridicule and contempt of those
who know not what moderation is, and who spend
their lives in making trifles serious things and serious
things trifles. But if we mean to come out from the
world we must not mind this. We must be " temperate "
even in lawful things, whatever others may think of
us. This is genuine Scriptural separation.

(ƒ) Last, but not least, he that desires to " come out
from the world, and be separate " must be *careful how
he allows himself in friendships, intimacies, and close
relationships with worldly people.*

We cannot help meeting many unconverted people
as long as we live. We cannot avoid having intercourse with them, and doing business with them,
unless "we go out of the world " (1 Cor. v. 10).
To treat them with the utmost courtesy, kindness, and
charity, whenever we do meet them, is a positive duty.
But acquaintance is one thing, and intimate friendship
is quite another. To seek their society without cause, to
choose their company, to cultivate intimacy with them,
is very dangerous to the soul. Human nature is so
constituted that we cannot be much with other people
without effect on our own character. The old proverb
will never fail to prove true : " Tell me with whom
a man chooses to live, and I will tell you what he is."

The Scripture says expressly, "He that walketh with wise men shall be wise; but a companion of fools shall be destroyed" (Prov. xiii. 20). If, then, a Christian, who desires to live consistently, chooses for his friends those who either do not care for their souls, or the Bible, or God, or Christ, or holiness, or regard them as of secondary importance, it seems to me impossible for him to prosper in his religion. He will soon find that their ways are not his ways, nor their thoughts his thoughts, nor their tastes his tastes; and that, unless they change, he must give up intimacy with them. In short, there must be separation. Of course such separation will be painful. But if we have to choose between the loss of a friend and the injury of our souls, there ought to be no doubt in our minds. If friends will not walk in the narrow way with us, we must not walk in the broad way to please them. But let us distinctly understand that to attempt to keep up close intimacy between a converted and an unconverted person, if both are consistent with their natures, is to attempt an impossibility.

The principle here laid down ought to be carefully remembered by all unmarried Christians in the choice of a husband or wife. I fear it is too often entirely forgotten. Too many seem to think of everything except religion in choosing a partner for life, or to suppose that it will come somehow as a matter of course. Yet when a praying, Bible-reading, God-fearing, Christ-loving, Sabbath-keeping Christian

P

marries a person who takes no interest whatever in
serious religion, what can the result be but injury
to the Christian, or immense unhappiness? Health
is not infectious, but disease is. As a general rule in
such cases, the good go down to the level of the
bad, and the bad do not come up to the level of the
good. The subject is a delicate one, and I do not
care to dwell upon it. But this I say confidently to
every unmarried Christian man or woman—if you
love your soul, if you do not want to fall away
and backslide, if you do not want to destroy your
own peace and comfort for life, resolve never to
marry any person who is not a thorough Christian,
whatever the resolution may cost you. You had
better die than marry an unbeliever. Stand to this
resolution, and let no one ever persuade you out of
it. Depart from this resolution, and you will find it
almost impossible to " come out and be separate."
You will find you have tied a mill-stone round your
own neck in running the race towards heaven ; and if
saved at last it will be " so as by fire." (1 Cor. iii. 15.)

I offer these six general hints to all who wish to
follow St. Paul's advice, and to come out from the
world and be separate. In giving them, I lay no
claim to infallibility; but I believe they deserve
consideration and attention. I do not forget that the
subject is full of difficulties, and that scores of doubtful
cases are continually arising in a Christian's course,
in which it is very hard to say what is the path of
duty, and how to behave. Perhaps the following bits

of advice may be found useful.—In all doubtful cases
we should first pray for wisdom and sound judgment.
If prayer is worth anything, it must be specially
valuable when we desire to do right, but do not see our
way. In all doubtful cases let us often try ourselves
by recollecting the eye of God. Should I go to such
and such a place, or do such and such a thing, if I
really thought God was looking at me? In all doubtful cases let us never forget the second advent of Christ
and the day of judgment. Should I like to be found
in such and such company, or employed in such and
such ways? Finally, in all doubtful cases let us find
out what the conduct of the holiest and best Christians
has been under similar circumstances. If we do not
clearly see our own way, we need not be ashamed to
follow good examples. I throw out these suggestions
for the use of all who are in difficulties about disputable
points, in the matter of separation from the world. I
cannot help thinking that they may help to untie
many knots, and solve many problems.

IV. I shall now conclude the whole subject by
trying to *show the secrets of real victory over the world.*
To come out from the world of course is not an
easy thing. It cannot be easy so long as human
nature is what it is, and a busy devil is always near
us. It requires a constant struggle and exertion; it
entails incessant conflict and self-denial; it often
places us in exact opposition to members of our own
families, to relations and neighbours; it sometimes

obliges us to do things which give great offence, and bring on us ridicule and petty persecution. It is precisely this which makes many hang back and shrink from decided religion. They know they are not right ; they know that they are not so " thorough " in Christ's service as they ought to be, and they feel uncomfortable and ill at ease. But the fear of man keeps them back. And so they linger on through life with aching, dissatisfied hearts—with too much religion to be happy in the world, and too much of the world to be happy in their religion. I fear this is a very common case, if the truth were known.

Yet there are some in every age who seem to get the victory over the world. They come out decidedly from its ways, and are unmistakably separate. They are independent of its opinions, and unshaken by its opposition. They move on like planets in an orbit of their own, and seem to rise equally above the world's smiles and frowns. And what are the secrets of their victory ? I will set them down.

(a) The first secret of victory over the world is a *right heart*. By that I mean a heart renewed, changed, and sanctified by the Holy Ghost—a heart in which Christ dwells, a heart in which old things have passed away, and all things become new. The grand mark of such a heart is the bias of its tastes and affections. The owner of such a heart no longer likes the world, and the things of the world, and therefore finds it no trial or sacrifice to give them up. He has no longer any appetite for the company, the conversation, the amusements, the occupations, the books which he once loved, and to "come out" from them seems natural to him. Great indeed is the expulsive power of a new principle! Just as the new spring-buds in a beech hedge push off the old leaves, and make them quietly fall to the ground, so does the new heart of a believer invariably effect his tastes and likings, and make him drop many things which he once loved and lived in, because he now likes them no more. Let him that wants to "come out from the world, and be separate," make sure first and foremost that he has got a new heart. If the heart is really right, everything else will be right in time. "If thine eye be single, thy whole body shall be full of light" (Matt. vi. 22.) If the affections are not right, there never will be right action.

(*b*) The second secret of victory over the world is a *lively practical faith* in unseen things. What saith the Scripture : "This is the victory that overcometh the world, even our faith "? (1 John v. 4). To attain and keep up the habit of looking steadily at invisible things, as if they were visible—to set before our minds every day, as grand realities, our souls, God, Christ heaven, hell, judgment, eternity—to cherish an abiding conviction that what we do not see is just as real as what we do see, and ten thousand times more important—this, this is one way to be conquerors over the world. This was the faith which made the noble army of saints, described in the eleventh chapter of Hebrews, obtain such a glorious testimony from the Holy

Ghost. They all acted under a firm persuasion that they had a real God, a real Saviour, and a real home in heaven, though unseen by mortal eyes. Armed with this faith a man regards this world as a shadow compared to the world to come, and cares little for its praise or blame, its enmity or its rewards. Let him that wants to come out from the world and be separate, but shrinks and hangs back for fear of the things seen, pray and strive to have this faith. " All things are possible to him that believeth" (Mark ix. 23). Like Moses, he will find it possible to forsake Egypt, seeing Him that is invisible. Like Moses, he will not care what he loses and who is displeased, because he sees afar off, like one looking though a telescope, a substantial recompense of reward. (Heb. i. 26).

(c) The third and last secret of victory over the world, is to attain and cultivate the *habit of boldly confessing Christ* on all proper occasions. In saying this I would not be mistaken. I want no one to blow a trumpet before him, and thrust his religion on others at all seasons. But I do wish to encourage all who strive to come out from the world to show their colours, and to act and speak out like men who are not ashamed to serve Christ. A steady, quiet assertion of our own principles, as Christians—an habitual readiness to let the children of the world see that we are guided by other rules than they are, and do not mean to swerve from them—a calm, firm, courteous maintenance of our own standard of things in every company—all this will insensibly form a habit within us, and make it comparatively easy to be a separate man. It will be hard at first, no doubt, and cost us many a struggle ; but the longer we go on, the easier will it be. Repeated acts of confessing Christ will produce habits. Habits once formed will produce a settled character. Our characters once known, we shall be saved much trouble. Men will know what to expect from us, and will count it no strange thing if they see us living the lives of separate peculiar people. He that grasps the nettle most firmly will always be less hurt than the man who touches it with a trembling hand. It as a great thing to be able to say "No" decidedly, but courteously, when asked to do anything which conscience says is wrong. He that shows his colours boldly from the first, and is never ashamed to let men see "whose he is and whom he serves," will soon find that he has overcome the world, and will be let alone. Bold confession is a long step towards victory.

It only remains for me now to conclude the whole subject with a few short words of application. The danger of the world ruining the soul, the nature of true separation from the world, the secrets of victory over the world, are all before the reader of this paper. I now ask him to give me his attention for the last time, while I try to say something directly for his personal benefit.

(1) My first word shall be *a question*. Reader, are you overcoming the world, or are you overcome by it ? Do you know what it is to come out from the world

and be separate, or are you yet entangled by it, and conform to it? If you have any desire to be saved, I entreat you to answer this question.

If you know nothing of "separation," I warn you affectionately that your soul is in great danger. The world passeth away; and they who cling to the world, and think only of the world, will pass away with it to everlasting ruin. Awake to know your peril before it be too late. Awake and flee from the wrath to come. The time is short. The end of all things is at hand. Tho shadows are lengthening. The sun is going down. The night cometh when no man can work. The great white throne will soon be set. The judgment will begin. The books will be opened. Awake, and come out from the world while it is called to-day.

Yet a little while, and there will be no more worldly occupations and worldly amusements—no more getting money and spending money—no more eating, and drinking, and feasting, and dressing, and ball-going, and theatres, and races, and cards, and gambling. Reader, what will you do when all these things have passed away for ever? How can you possibly be happy in an eternal heaven, where holiness is all in all, and worldliness has no place? Oh, consider these things, and be wise! Awake, and break the chains which the world has thrown around you. Awake and flee from the wrath to come.

(2) My second word shall be *a counsel.* Reader, if you want to come out from the world, but know not what to do, take the advice which I give you this

day. Begin by applying direct, as a penitent sinner, to our Lord Jesus Christ, and put your case in his hands. Pour out your heart before him. Tell Him your whole story, and keep nothing back. Tell Him that you are a sinner wanting to be saved from the world, the flesh, and the devil, and entreat Him to save you.

That blessed Saviour " gave Himself for our sins, that He might deliver us from this present evil world " (Gal. i. 2). He knows what the world is, for He lived in it thirty and three years. He knows what the difficulties of a man are, for He was made man for our sakes, and dwelt among men. High in heaven, at the right hand of God, He is able to save to the uttermost all who come to God by Him—able to keep us from the evil of the world while we are still living in it—able to give us power to become the Sons of God—able to keep us from falling—able to make us more than conquerors. Reader, once more I say, Go direct to Christ with the prayer of faith, and put yourself wholly and unreservedly in His hands. Hard as it may seem to you now to come out from the world and be separate, you shall find that with Jesus nothing is impossible. You, even you, shall overcome the world.

(3) My third and last word shall be *encouragement*. Reader, if you have learned by experience what it is to come out from the world, I can only say to you, Take comfort, and persevere. You are in the right road ; you have no cause to be afraid. The everlasting hills are in sight. Your salvation is nearer

than when you believed. Take comfort and
press on.

No doubt you have had many a battle, and made
many a false step. You have sometimes felt ready to
faint, and been half disposed to go back to Egypt. But
your Master has never entirely left you, and He will
never suffer you to be tempted above that you are able
to bear. Then persevere steadily in your separation
from the world, and never be ashamed of standing alone.
Settle it firmly in your mind that the most decided
Christians are always the happiest, and remember that
no one ever said at the end of his course that he had
been too holy, and lived too near to God.

Hear, last of all, what is written in the Scriptures of
truth :

" Whosoever shall confess Me before men, him shall
the Son of man also confess before the angels of God "
(Luke xii. 8).

" There is no man that hath left house, or brethren,
or sisters, or father, or mother, or wife, or children, or
lands, for my sake, and the gospel's,

" But he shall receive an hundredfold now in this
time, houses, and brethren, and sisters, and mothers,
and children, and lands, with persecutions ; and in the
world to come eternal life " (Mark x. 29, 30).

" Cast not away therefore your confidence, which hath
great recompence of reward.

" For ye have need of patience, that, after ye have
done the will of God, ye might receive the promise.

" For yet a little while, and He that shall come will come, and will not tarry" (Heb. x. 35—37).

Christian reader, those words were written and spoken for your sake. Lay hold on them, and never forget them. Persevere to the end, and never be ashamed of coming out from the world, and being separate. Be sure it brings its own reward.

"WHAT CANST THOU KNOW?"

" WHAT CANST THOU KNOW ? "

———o———

"Canst thou by searching find out God? canst thou find out the Almighty unto perfection ? It is as high as heaven ; what canst thou do ? deeper than hell ; what canst thou know ?— JOB XI. 7, 8.

THESE striking words came from the lips of Zophar the Naamathite, one of the three friends who came to comfort the patriarch Job in his affliction. Those worthy men, no doubt, meant well ; and their sympathy is deserving of all praise in a cold and unfeeling world. But they completely misunderstood the case before them, and so proved "physicians of no value." They only irritated the poor sufferer, and added to his troubles. Nevertheless, it is undeniable that they said many wise and excellent things, and of these the passage which heads this paper is one.

The verses before us contain four weighty questions. Two of them we certainly cannot answer, but two we can. A little brief discussion of the whole subject to which the text points appears suitable to the times in which we live.

Our lot is cast in a day when a wave of unbelief is passing over the world, like a wave of fever, cholera, diphtheria, or plague. It is vain to deny it. Every intelligent observer of the times knows that it is so. I do not say for a moment that the advance of science necessarily makes men unbelievers. Nothing is further from my thoughts. I welcomed the visit of the British Association to Southport in the diocese of Liverpool, Lancashire, and I am thankful for every addition to our knowledge which its leaders annually announce. I doubt whether formal, organized, systematic, reasoning infidelity is so common as many suppose. But I do say that there is in the air of these times a disposition to question everything in revealed religion, and to suspect that science and revelation cannot be reconciled. The faith of many church-goers and professing Christians seems cold, and languid, and torpid. They are continually harping on petty modern objections to Scripture.—" Are such and such things in the Bible really quite true? Do not some clever and learned people say we should not believe them?" This is the kind of mischievous talk which is often heard in many quarters. To supply some simple antidotes to this sceptical spirit, to show the unreasonableness of it, to nerve and invigorate the Christian, to make him see the strength of his position, to help him to get rid of a doubting spirit, and to enable him to grasp his old creed more tightly than ever—these are the objects I have in view in this paper.

I. First, and foremost, a wise Christian ought always to admit that *there are many things in Bible religion which of necessity we cannot fully under-*

stand. The Book of Revelation, the Book of God, contains much which, like God Himself, we cannot "find out to perfection.'"

The catalogue of these hard things is not a small one, and I shall only supply a few leading instances. I will mention the Mosaic account of creation,—the fall and entrance of sin into the world,—the doctrine of the Trinity,—the incarnation of Christ,—the atonement for sin made by Christ's death,—the personality and work of the Holy Spirit,—the inspiration of Scripture,—the reality of miracles,—the use and efficacy of prayer,—the precise nature of the future state,—the resurrection of the body after death:— each and all of these subjects, I say, contains much that we cannot fully explain, because it is above the reach of our faculties. No Christian of common sense, I believe, would pretend to deny it. The humblest child could ask questions about each of them which the wisest theologian in Christendom could never answer.

But what of it? Does it follow that we are to believe *nothing* about a subject, and to reject it altogether, because we do not understand everything about it? Is this fair and reasonable? Is this the way that we deal with our children when we require them to begin the study of mathematics, or any other branch of education? Do we allow our boys to say, "I will learn nothing till I understand everything?" Do we not require them to take many things on trust, and to begin by simply believing? "I speak as to wise men, judge ye what I say."

The plain truth is that to refuse to believe Christian doctrines because they are *above* our reason, and we cannot fully understand them, is only one among many proofs of man's natural pride and arrogance. We are all, at our best, poor, weak, defective creatures. Our power of grasping any subject, and seeing all round it, is extremely small. Our education rarely goes on for more than twenty years, and is often very shallow and superficial. After twenty-five most of us add little to our knowledge. We plunge into some profession in which we have little time for thought or reading, and are absorbed and distracted by the business and cares of life. By the time we are seventy, our memories and intellects begin to fail, and in a few years we are carried to our graves and see corruption. And is it likely, or probable, or reasonable to suppose that such a creature as this can ever understand perfectly the Eternal and Almighty God, or the communications that God has made to man? Is it not rather certain that there will be many things about God and revelation that he cannot, from his very nature, comprehend. I will not insult my readers by asking for a reply. I assert, without hesitation, that no Christian ever need be ashamed of admitting that there are many things in revealed religion which he does not fully understand, and does not pretend to explain. Yet he believes them fully, and lives in this belief.

After all, when a Christian meets one of those few men of science who profess to believe nothing in religion which he cannot fully *understand*, he would do well to ask him a simple question. Has he ever investigated the facts and doctrines of the Bible, which he says are incredible, with the same careful pains which he exercises when he uses his microscope, his telescope, his spectroscope, his dissecting knife, or his chemical apparatus? I doubt it extremely. I venture to believe that if some scientific infidels would examine the Book of God with the same reverent analysis with which they daily examine the Book of Nature, they would find that the things "hard to be understood" are not so many and inscrutable as they now suppose, and that the things plain and easy are a wide field which richly repays cultivation. That we "cannot find out the Almighty to perfection" let us always admit. But let us never admit that we can find out nothing, and are justified in neglecting Him.

II. The second point which I wish to bring forward is this. A wise Christian ought always to remember *that there are countless things in the material world around us which we do not fully understand.* There are deep things in the Book of Nature as well as in the Bible. Its pages contain hard knots and mysteries as well as the pages of the Book of God. In short, science contains its hard things as well as faith.

I am quite sure that the wisest and most learned men of science would be the most ready to admit the truth of what I have just said. If anything has specially characterized them in every age, it has been their deep humility. The more they have known the more they have confessed the limited extent of their knowledge. The memorable language which Sir Isaac Newton is said to have used towards the end of his life ought never to be forgotten:—"I have been nothing more than a little child who has picked up a few shells and pebbles on the shore of the ocean of truth."

How little, to begin with, do we know about the heaven over our heads, or the earth under our feet! The sun, the moon, the planets, the fixed stars, the comets, can all supply deep questions which the wisest astronomers cannot answer. Yet, for all this, who but a fool would despise the work of Newton, and Halley, and Herschel, and Arago, and Airey? The age of the globe on which we live, the date and cause of the various convulsions it has gone through, long before man was created, the duration of the periods between each change of climate and temperature, what wise geologists will dare to speak positively of such subjects as these? They may speculate, and guess, and propound theories. But how often their conclusions have been overthrown! Yet who would dare to say that Buckland, and Sedgwick, and Phillips, and Lyell, and Murchison, and Owen had written nothing worth notice?

How little can we account for the action of some deadly poisons, and especially in the case of snake-bites, and hydrophobia! The virus of a mad dog's bite will often remain dormant in the system for months, and then become active, and defy all medical treatment. But no one can explain what that virus is. The deaths caused by snake-bites in India are reported to be about 20,000 a year. Yet to this day the precise nature of the cobra's venom has baffled all chemical analysis, and once received into the human body, the most skilful doctors find they cannot prevent that venom causing death. But what man in his senses would conclude that chemistry and medicine are unworthy of respect, and that Liebig, and Fresenius, or Hervey, and Hunter, and Jenner, and Watson, have conferred no benefit on the world?

How little can men of science account for all the phenomena of light, heat, electricity, magnetism, and chemical action! How many problems lie under the words, "matter, force, energy," which no one has solved! Far be it from me to disparage the extraordinary advances which physical science has made in this generation. But I am quite certain that its leading students, from Faraday downwards, will confess that there are many things which they cannot explain.

How little do we know about earthquakes, volcanic eruptions, hurricanes, and epidemics! They come suddenly, like the recent awful catastrophes at Ischia and Java, or the historic events at Pompeii and Lisbon. They cause immense destruction of life and property. But why they come when they do come, and what laws regulate them, so that the inhabitants of a country may be prepared for them, even in this enlightened nineteenth century, we are totally and entirely ignorant. We can only lay our hands on our mouths and be still. (See Editorial note, page 251.)

How little, to bring matters to a familiar point, how less than little, or nothing in reality, can we explain the connection between our minds and bodies! Who can tell me why a sense of shame makes the little child's face turn red, or a sense of fear makes the same face turn pale? Who can tell me how my will affects my members, and what it is that makes me walk, or move, or lift my hand whenever I wish? Nobody ever did explain it, and nobody ever will. It is one of the many things that baffle all inquiry.

Now what shall we say to the facts I have adduced? That they are facts I am sure no man of common-sense will deny. If I were to say to a man of science, "I do not believe any of your conclusions, because there are many hard things in the Book of Nature which you cannot explain," I should be acting very foolishly. I shall do nothing of the kind. I have not the slightest sympathy with those weak-kneed Christians, who seem to think that science and religion can never harmonize, and that they must always scowl and look askance at one another, like two quarrelsome dogs. On the contrary, I shall always hail the annual discoveries of physical science with a hearty welcome. For the continual progress of its students by experiment and observation, and for their annual accumulation of facts, I am deeply thankful. I am not the least afraid that science will ever finally contradict Christian theology (though it may appear to do so for a season), if students of science will only be logical. I only fear that, in their zeal, they are sometimes apt to forget that it is most illogical to draw a general conclusion from a particular premise,—to build houses of theories without foundations. I am firmly convinced that the words of God's mouth, and the works of God's hands, will never be found really to contradict one another. When they appear to do so, I am content to wait. Time will untie the knot.

I do not forget that some young philosophers are fond of talking of the "Laws of Nature," and of saying that they cannot reconcile them with the Bible. They tell us that these "laws" are unchangeable, and that the miracles and supernatural parts of Revelation, which seem to contradict the laws of nature, are therefore incredible. But these philosophers would do well to remember that it is not at all certain that we know all the Laws of Nature, and that higher, and deeper Laws may not yet be discovered. At any rate they must own that some of the existing "Laws" were not known and received three or four centuries ago. But surely, if that is the case, we may fairly assume that many other "Laws" may yet be found out, and that many problems which we cannot solve now will be solved hereafter. (See note A., p. 252.)

Two things, however, I must say, before leaving this part of my paper.

(a) On the one side, I appeal to those few men of science who turn away from Christianity, and refuse to believe, because of the hard things which its creed requires them to believe. I ask them whether this is just and fair. We do not turn away from physical science because it contains many things which they themselves admit they cannot explain. On the contrary, we bid them God speed, and wish success to their researches and investigations. But in return we ask them to deal honestly with Christianity. We admit that it contains difficulties, like physical science; but we cannot allow that this is any reason why it should be rejected altogether.

(*b*) On the other side, I appeal to those timid Christians whose faith is shaken by the attacks which men of science sometimes make on their creed, and are ready to throw down their arms and run away. I ask them whether this is not weak, and cowardly, and foolish? I bid them remember that the difficulties of the sceptical man of science are just as great as those of the Christian. I entreat them to stand firm and not be afraid. Let us frankly admit that there are deep things and " hard to be understood " in our creed. But let us steadily maintain that this is no proof that it is not true and not worthy of all acceptation.

III. The third and last point to which I shall ask the attention of my readers is this. *While it is true that we cannot find out the Almighty to perfection, it is not true to say that we can find out nothing at all in religion.* On the contrary, we know many things which are enough to make unbelief and agnosticism inexcusable.

What, then, do we know? Let me mention a few facts which no intelligent person can pretend to deny

(*a*) We find ourselves living in a world full of sorrow, pain, strife, and wickedness, which no advance of science, learning, or civilization, is able to prevent. We see around us daily proof that we are all, one after another, going out of this world to the grave. Humbling as the thought is, we are all dying daily, and these bodies, which we take such pains to feed, and clothe, and comfort, must see corruption. It is the same all over the globe. Death comes to all men and women alike, of every name, and nation, and people, and tongue; and neither rank, nor riches, nor intellect, can grant exemption. Dust we are, and to dust we return. At any rate we know this.

(b) We find, moreover, that all over the world the vast majority of mankind have a settled, rooted, inward feeling, that this life is not all, that there is a future state, and an existence beyond the grave. The absence of this feeling is the exception. There it is. Assyria, Egypt, Greece, Rome, Hindustan, China, Mexico, and the darkest heathen tribes, as a general rule, are agreed on this point, however strange and diverse their ideas of God, and religion, and the soul. Will any one tell me that we do not know this?

(c) We find, moreover, that the only thing which has ever enabled men and women to look forward to the future without fear, and has given them peace in life, and hope in death, is that religion which Jesus Christ brought into the world nearly nineteen hundred years ago, and of which Christ Himself is the sun, and centre, and root, and foundation. Christ, I say emphatically,—Christ and His Divinity,—Christ and His atoning death,—Christ and His resurrection,—Christ and His life in heaven. Yes! that very religion of Christ which some tell us they cannot receive because of the mysteries and difficulties of its creed, has made the deepest moral mark on mankind that has been made since man was created. Nothing called religion, whether Classic heathenism, or Buddhism, or Confucianism, or Mahometanism, has ever produced effects on consciences and conduct, which can bear comparison for a moment with the effects produced by Christianity. The changes which have taken place in the state of the world before Christ and the world after Christ, and the difference at this day between those parts of the globe where the Bible is read, and those where it is not known, are great patent facts which have never been explained away. The holiest lives and the happiest deaths which have been seen on the earth for eighteen centuries have been the result of the supernatural theology of the Bible, of faith in and of obedience to Christ, and the story of the cross. I challenge any one to deny this.

(d) We find, above all, that the Historic Founder of Christianity, Jesus Christ Himself, is a great fact which has been before the world for eighteen centuries, and has completely baffled all the efforts of infidels and non-Christians to explain it away. No sceptical writer has ever given a satisfactory answer to the question—"Who was Christ? Whence did He come?" The super-human purity of His life, confessed even by men like Rousseau and Napoleon (See note B, p. 254),—the super-human wisdom of His teaching,—the super-human mystery of His death,—the inexplicable incident of His resurrection,—the undeniable influence which His apostles obtained for His doctrines, without the aid of money or arms,—all these are simple matters of history, and demand the attention of every honest man who really wishes to inquire into the great subject of religion. They are indisputable facts in the annals of the world. Let those who dare deny them.

Now what shall we say to these facts? That they are facts I think no one of average intelligence can possibly deny. I assert that they form a mass of evidence in favour of Christianity which cannot be safely neglected by any honest mind. "What canst thou know?" says Zophar. I answer, we know enough to justify every Christian in resting his soul calmly and confidently on the revelation which God has given us of Himself, and of Christ, in His Bible. That revelation is supported by such an enormous mass of probable evidence that we may safely trust its truth. I answer, furthermore, that we "know" enough to warrant us in urging every sceptic to consider seriously, as a prudent man, whether he is not occupying a very dangerous and untenable position. Probabilities are all against him; and probabilities, in the vast majority of things, are the only guide of choice and action. He cannot say that the witness of eighteen centuries is so weak and worthless that it deserves no attention. On the contrary, it is so strong that, if he cannot explain it away, he ought either to throw down the arms of his unbelief, or to avow that he is not open to reason. In a word, he is not willing to be convinced. He has shut his eyes, and is determined not to open them. Well might our Lord say, "If they hear not Moses and the prophets, neither will they be persuaded, though one rose from the dead." Well might He "marvel at unbelief" (Luke xvi. 31. Mark vi. 6).

I shall now conclude this paper with two general remarks which I commend to the attention of all who read it.

1. For one thing, let me try to show *the true causes of* a vast amount of the unbelief of the present day.

That there is a good deal of unbelief in this age it is vain to deny. The number of people who attend no place of worship, and seem to have no religion, is very considerable. A vague kind of scepticism or agnosticism is one of the commonest spiritual diseases in this generation. It meets us at every turn, and crops up in every company. Like the Egyptian plague of frogs, it makes its way into every family and home, and there seems no keeping it out. Among high and low, and rich and poor, in town and country, in Universities and manufacturing towns, in castles and in cottages, you will continually find some form of unbelief. It is no longer a pestilence that walketh in darkness, but a destruction that wasteth at noonday. It is even considered clever and intellectual, and a mark of a thoughtful mind. Society seems leavened with it. He that avows his belief of *everything* contained in the Bible must make up his mind in many companies to be smiled at contemptuously, and thought an ignorant and weak man.

(*a*) Now there is no doubt that, as I have already said, the seat of unbelief in some persons is *the head*. They refuse to accept anything which they cannot understand, or which seems above their reason. Inspiration, Miracles, the Trinity, the Incarnation, the Atonement, the Holy Spirit, the Resurrection, the Future State, all these mighty verities are viewed with cold indifference as disputable points, if not absolutely rejected. "Can we entirely explain them? Can we satisfy their reasoning faculties about them?" If not they must be excused if they stand in doubt. What they cannot fully understand, they tell us they cannot fully believe, and so they never observe the Sabbath, and never exhibit any religion while they live, though, strangely enough, they like to be buried with religious forms when they die.

(*b*) But while I admit this, I am equally certain that with some the real seat of unbelief is *the heart*. They love the sins and habits of life which the Bible condemns, and are determined not to give them up. They take refuge from an uneasy conscience by trying to persuade themselves that the old Book is not true. The measure of their creed is their affection. Whatever condemns their natural inclinations, they refuse to believe. The famous Lord Rochester, once a profligate and an infidel, but at last a true penitent, is recorded to have said to Bishop Burnet, as he drew near his end, "It is not reason, but a bad life, which is the great argument against the Bible." A true and weighty saying! Many, I am persuaded, profess that they do not believe, because they know, if they did believe, they must give up their favourite sins.

(c) Last, but not least, with far the greater number of people the seat of unbelief is a lazy, indolent *will*. They dislike all kind of trouble. Why should they deny themselves, and take pains about Bible-reading and praying, and Sabbath observance, and diligent watchfulness over thoughts, and words, and actions, when, after all, it is not quite certain that the Bible is true? This, I have little doubt, is the form of unbelief which prevails most frequently among young people. They are not agitated by intellectual difficulties. They are often not the slaves of any special lusts or passions, and live tolerably decent lives. But deep down in their hearts there is a disinclination to make up their minds, and to be decided about anything in religion. And so they drift down the stream of life like dead fish, and float helplessly on, and are tossed to and fro, hardly knowing what they believe. And while they would shrink from telling you they are not Christians, they are without any backbone in their Christianity.

Now, whether head, or heart, or will, be in fault, it is some comfort to remember that there is probably less of real, downright, reasoning unbelief than there appears to be. Thousands, we may be sure, do not in their heart of hearts believe all that they say with their lips. Many a sceptical saying is nothing more than a borrowed article, picked up and retailed by him who says it, because it sounds clever, while, in reality, it is not the language of his inner man.

Sorrow, and sickness, and affliction, often bring out the strange fact that so-called sceptics are not sceptics at all, and that many *talk* scepticism merely from a desire to seem clever, and to win the temporary applause of clever men. That there is an immense amount of unbelief in the present day I make no question; but that much of it is mere show and pretence is, to my mind, as clear as noonday. No man, I think, can do pastoral work, and come to close quarters with souls, visit the sick, and attend the dying, without coming to that conclusion.

The parting advice I offer to heart sceptics is simply this. Let me entreat you to *deal honestly with your soul about secret sins.* Are you sure there is not some bad habit, or lust, or passion, which, almost insensibly to yourself, you would like to indulge, if it were not for some remaining scruples? Are you quite sure that your doubts do not arise from a desire to get rid of restraint? You would like, if you could, to do something the Bible forbids, and you are looking about for reasons for disregarding the Bible. Oh! if this is the case with any of my readers, awake to a sense of your danger! Break the chains which are gradually closing round you. Pluck out the right eye, if need be; but never be the servant of sin. I repeat that the secret love of some vicious indulgence is the real beginning of a vast amount of infidelity.

The parting advice I offer to lazy sceptics is this. Let me entreat you to *deal honestly with your souls about the use of means for acquiring religious knowledge.* Can you lay your hand on your heart and say that you really take pains to find out what is truth? Do not be ashamed to pray for light. Do not be ashamed of reading some leading book about the Creeds and the Confession of your own Church, and, above all, do not be ashamed of regularly studying the text of your Bible. Thousands, I am persuaded, in this day, know nothing of the Holy Book which they affect to despise, and are utterly ignorant of the real nature of that Christianity which they pretend they cannot believe. Let not that be the case with you. That famous "honest doubt," which many say is better than "half the creeds," is a pretty thing to talk about. But I venture a strong suspicion that much of the scepticism of the present day, if sifted and analyzed, would be found to spring from utter ignorance of the primary evidences of Christianity .

2. The other concluding remark which I will make is this. I will try to explain *the reason why so many professing Christians are continually frightened* and shaken in their minds by doubts about the truth of Christianity.

That this is the case of many I have a very strong impression. I suspect there are thousands of Sabbath-keeping, church-going Christians who would repudiate with indignation the charge of scepticism, and yet are constantly troubled about the truth of Christianity. Some new book, or lecture, or sermon, appears from the pen of men like Darwin or Colenso, and at once these worthy people are scared and panic-stricken, and run from clergyman to clergyman to pour out their anxieties and fears, as if the very ark of God was in danger. "Can these new ideas be really true?" they cry. "Must we really give up the Old Testament, and the flood, and the miracles, and the resurrection of Christ? Alas! alas! what shall we do?" In short, like Ahaz, their "hearts are moved, as the trees of the wood are moved with the wind" (Isaiah vii. 2).

Now what is the cause of this readiness to give way to doubts? Why are so many alarmed about the faith of eighteen centuries, and frightened out of their wits by attacks which no more shake the evidences of Christianity than the scratch of a pin shakes the great Pyramid of Egypt.

The reason is soon told. The answer lies in a nutshell. The greater part of modern Christians are utterly ignorant of the evidences of Christianity, and the enormous difficulties of infidelity. The education of the vast majority of people on these subjects is wretchedly meagre and superficial, or it is no education at all. Not one in a hundred church-goers, probably, has ever read a page of Leslie, or Leland, or Watson, or Butler, or Paley, or Chalmers, or M'Ilvaine, or Daniel Wilson, or Porteus, or Whately. What wonder if the minds of such people are like a city without walls, and utterly unable to resist the attacks of the most commonplace infidelity, much less of the refined and polished scepticism of these latter days.

The remedy for this state of things is patent and plain. Every professing Christian should arm his mind with some elementary knowledge of the evidences of revealed religion and the difficulties of infidelity, and so be ready to give a reason for the faith that he professes. He ought not merely to read and love his Bible, but to be able to tell any one why he believes the Bible to be true. Ministers should preach occasionally on evidences. It was one of that great man Cecil's counsels to a clergyman, "In your sermons never forget the infidel." Schools, Colleges, and Universities, which make any pretence to be Christian, should never altogether leave out evidences in their scheme of instruction for the young. In short, if we want the coming generation to hold fast Christianity, we must provide them with defensive armour.

With these two remarks I close my paper. Thank God! we travel on to a world where there is no ignorance, no scepticism, and no doubt. We shall soon see as we have been seen, and know as we have been known. Alas! What a waking up remains for many the moment the last breath is drawn! There is no unbelief in the grave. Voltaire now knows whether there is a sin-hating God; and David Hume now knows whether there is an endless hell. The infant of days, by merely dying, acquires a knowledge which the subtlest philosophers, while on earth, profess their inability to attain. The dead Hottentot knows more than the living Socrates. To that future world the true Christian may look forward calmly, confidently, and without fear. He that has Christ in his heart, and the Bible in his head, is standing on a rock, and has no cause to be afraid. "Therefore, my beloved brethren, let us be steadfast, unmoveable, always abounding in the work of the Lord, knowing that our labour is not in vain in the Lord" (1 Cor. xv. 58). If we cannot "find out the Almighty to perfection," we can know enough to give us peace in life, and hope in death. What we "know" 'et us hold fast.

One thing at least is certain. If we "KNOW" little we can DO much. Is it not written, "If any man will do His will, he shall know of the doctrine, whether it be of God."—"The secret things belong unto the Lord our God: but those things which are revealed belong unto us, and to our children for ever, that we may do all the words of this law" (John vii. 17; Deut. xxix. 29).

EDITORIAL NOTE.

Science has moved forward since Bishop Ryle penned these lines: still his reasoning is valid for to-day. The Bacterial or Germ Theory of disease has not cleared up all the mysteries connected with its origin and nature. Again, as regards the ultimate constitution of matter and force, the conclusions which held ground among scientific men until lately have been completely overthrown by the discovery of the remarkable metal radium, and the study of its phenomena. Lastly, the more recent convulsions, volcanic and seismic, which occurred at St. Pierre, San Francisco, and Messina, accompanied as these have been with tremendous loss of life, prove that the progress of science still leaves the human race as helpless as ever in the presence of this class of calamity.

NOTE A. TO PAGE 239 .

The following page from Carlyle's "Sartor Resartus" contains so many useful thoughts about miracles and the so-called laws of nature that I make no apology for giving it to the readers of this paper, and commending it to their attention. In giving it I must not be supposed to be a wholesale admirer of the writer, or of his peculiar style.

" ' But is not a Miracle simply a violation of the Laws of Nature '? ask several. Whom I answer by this new question, What are the Laws of Nature? To me, perhaps, the rising of one from the dead were no violation of these Laws, but a confirmation; were some far deeper Law, now first penetrated into, and by Spiritual Force, even as the rest have all been, brought to bear on us with its Material force.

"Here, too, some may inquire, not without astonishment, ' On what ground shall one, that can make iron swim, come and declare that therefore he can teach religion?' To us, truly, of the nineteenth century, such declaration were inapt enough, which, nevertheless, to our fathers, of the first century, was full of meaning.

"But is it not the deepest Law of Nature that she be constant?' cries an illuminated class. ' Is not the Machine of the Universe fixed to move by unalterable rules?' Probable enough, good friends; nay, I, too,

must believe that the God whom ancient inspired men
assert to be 'without variableness or shadow of turning' does indeed never change; that Nature, that the
Universe, which no one whom it so pleases can be
prevented from calling a Machine, does move by the
most unalterable rules. And now of you, too, I make
the old inquiry, 'What those same unalterable rules,
forming the complete statute book of Nature, may
possibly be?'

"'They stand written in our Works of Science' say
you; 'in the accumulated records of man's experience?' Was man with his experience present at the
Creation, then, to see how it all went on? Have any
deepest scientific individuals yet dived down to the
foundation of the Universe, and gauged everything
there? Did the Maker take them into His counsel,
that they read His ground-plan of the incomprehen-
sible All; and can say, 'This stands marked therein,
and no more than this'? Alas! not in anyone!
These scientific individuals have been nowhere but
where we also are, have seen some handbreadths
deeper than we see into the Deep that is infinite, without bottom, as without shore.

"System of Nature! To the wisest man, wide as
is his vision, Nature remains of quite *infinite* depth,
of quite infinite expansion; and all experience thereof
limits itself to some few computed centuries and
measured square miles. The course of Nature's
phases, on this our little fraction of a Planet, is
partially known to us: but who knows what deeper
courses these depend on, what infinitely larger Cycle

(of causes) our little Epicycle revolves on? To the Minnow every cranny, and pebble, and quality, and accident of its little native Creek may have become familiar; but does the Minnow understand the Ocean Tides and periodic currents, the Trade-winds, and Monsoons, and Moon's Eclipses; by all which the condition of its little is regulated, and may, from time to time (*un*miraculously enough) be quite overset and reversed? Such a Minnow is Man; his Creek this Planet Earth, his Ocean the immeasurable All, his Monsoons and Periodic Currents the Mysterious Course of Providence through Æons of Æons!"

NOTE B. TO PAGE 242.

The language of Rousseau about Christ, referred to in this sermon, is so remarkable that I think it may be useful to give it in its entirety:

"Is it possible that He, whose history the Gospel records, can be but a mere man? Does He speak in the tone of an enthusiast, or of an ambitious sectary? What mildness, what purity in His manners! What touching grace in His instructions, what elevation in His maxims! What profound wisdom in His discourses! What presence of mind! What ingenuity, and what justness in His answers! What government of His passions! What prejudice, what blindness or ill faith must that be which dares to compare Socrates, the son of Sophroniscus, with the Son of Mary! What a difference between the two! Socrates dying without pain, without disgrace, easily sustains his part to the last. The death of Socrates philosophizing tranquilly with his friends is the mildest that could be desired: that of Jesus expiring in torments, injured, mocked, cursed by all the people, is the most horrible that can be feared. Socrates, taking the empoisoned cup, blesses him who presents it to him with tears. Jesus, in the midst of a frightful punishment, prays for his enraged executioners. Yes, if the life and death of Socrates are those of a sage, the life and death of Jesus are those of a God." —*Emile Rousseau.*

The words of Napoleon at St. Helena towards the close of his life were these: "I know men, and I tell you that Jesus is not a man."